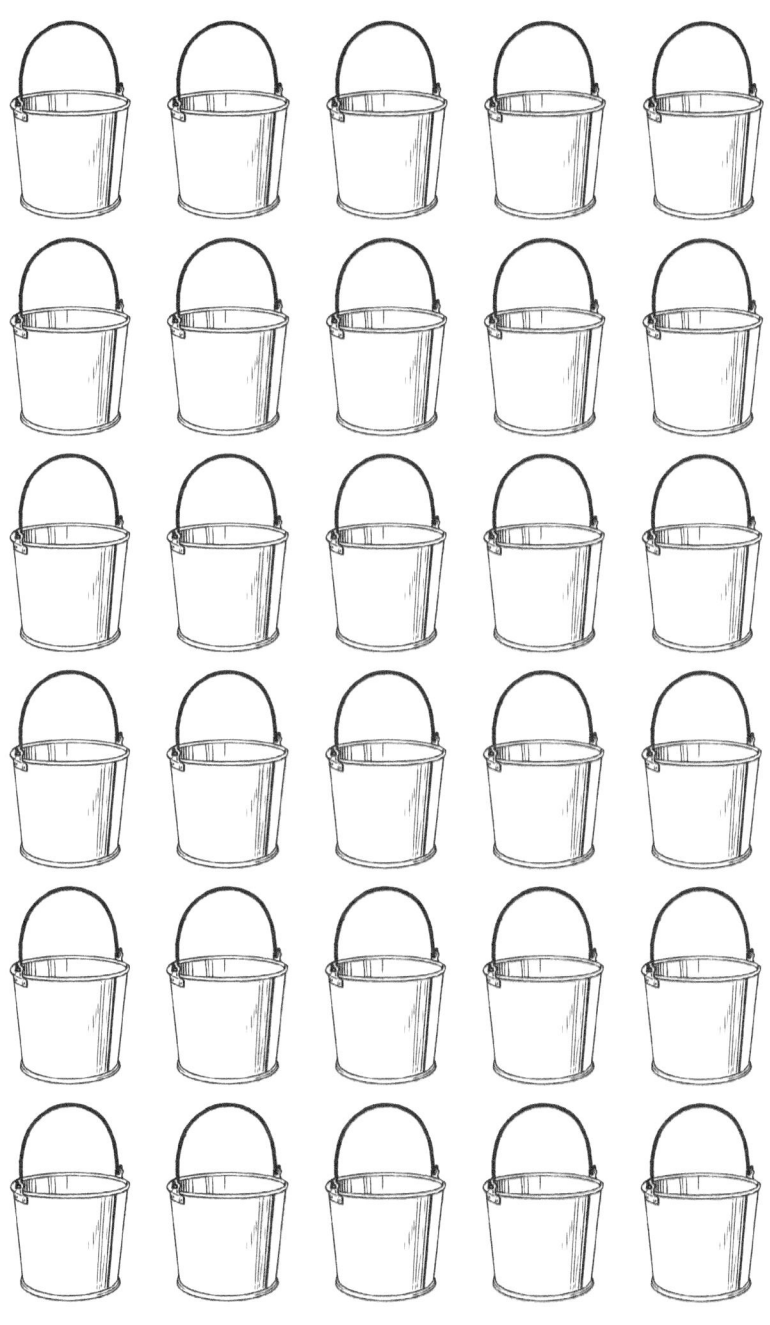

Pure Slush Books

# 2014

## January

### Vol. 1

a Pure Slush book

Pure
Slush

*2014 January Vol. 1* is edited by Matt Potter and
published by Pure Slush, December 2013.

Cover photograph copyright © of Amalrik Dumas
http://www.amalrik.fr

ISBN: 978-1-925101-03-4

You can find *Pure Slush* at http://pureslush.webs.com

Copies of all *Pure Slush* publications can be bought
at http://pureslush.webs.com/store.htm

All queries re *Pure Slush* can be made
via email to edpureslush@live.com.au

A note on differences in punctuation and spelling

*Pure Slush* proudly features (both online and in print) writers from all over the English-speaking world. Some speak and write English as their first language, while for others, it's their second or third or even fourth language. Naturally, across all versions of English, there are differences in punctuation and spelling, and even in meaning. These differences are reflected in the stories *Pure Slush* publishes, and it accounts for any differences in punctuation, spelling and meaning found within these pages.

stories by

Guilie Castillo-Oriard

Townsend Walker

Derek Osborne

Gloria Garfunkel

John Wentworth Chapin

Lynn Beighley

Andrew Stancek

Rachel Ambrose

Gill Hoffs

Susan Tepper

Jessica McHugh

Shane Simmons

Michelle Elvy

Len Kuntz

Michael Webb

James Claffey

Gwendolyn Joyce Mintz

Stephen V. Ramey

Gay Degani

Sally-Anne Macomber

Mandy Nicol

Margaret Bingel

Darryl Price

Teresa Burns Gunther

Matt Potter

Gary Percesepe

Nathaniel Tower

Kimberlee Smith

Vanessa Weibler Paris

Joanne Jagoda

h. l. nelson

for

Rosie,

Madame La Mush,

she with the sweet sweet face


M.P.

# Preface

Call me crazy but I thought gathering together 365 stories would be fun!

So this is the idea ... a year of stories, one story a day for an entire year, all written like they're happening right now as you read them.

And each writer has a set day each month, where the reader can watch / read about / discover again / enjoy characters' lives as they unfold across the year. So Guilie Castillo−Oriard always has the 1st, Townsend Walker always has the 2nd, Derek Osborne always has the 3rd day of the month, etc, right through to h. l. nelson who has the 31$^{st}$.

So you have the beginning in your hands.

Meet you at the end.

Matt Potter, editor *Pure Slush*, December 2013

Wednesday, 1ˢᵗ January 2014

# The Miracle of Small Things

## by Guilie Castillo–Oriard

There's no stillness like the stillness of Curaçao on New Year's Day. Pointless tropical sun on deserted asphalt, every business shuttered, everything forlorn. Not even trash stirs: the wind is on furlough too. There's also no New Year's Eve like Curaçao's, which might explain the stillness. But to Luis Villalobos it feels like the cold shoulder of the world.

Luis has just ruined his life.

He brakes for a red light even though his black Wrangler Rubicon is the only vehicle in sight. He's seen no one, not even on foot, since pulling out of Milena's carport. Feels surreal, a desolate dimension he's crossed into by accident. In a sense it is: utterly different from Mexico City, London, Hong Kong, anywhere else he's lived. But he isn't here by accident.

He was lured, away from the plum at the legendary Cabrera y Machado of Mexico City, to this tiny speck of land no one in the civilized world can or wants to find on a map, by the one–in–a–million carrot of replacing Milena as MD next year. Would've been just the start; Luis's ambitions know no limits. Apparently, his intelligence does.

He could've had his pick of sexy inebriated females last night; they all seemed to find him irresistible. Stepan told him to enjoy it, that new–kid–on–the–office–block popularity. "You single? Go for it, bicho. Won't last forever." Wearing his new colleague's permission like a groupie brandishing a backstage

17

pass, Luis went for it. With the Managing Director of Ehrlich Fiduciary's Curaçao branch.

The boss.

Luis taps his forehead against the steering wheel – softly; a headache is already barreling down the helpless conduits between neurons. Even with the car's A/C at full blast, he catches whiffs of Milena's Carolina Herrera.

In a world where profit justifies not just means but everything else, there is only one taboo: sex with a colleague. That's the sleaze line. Sex with the boss – well. Professional hara–kiri, just not quite so swift.

Luis runs his tongue over his teeth and checks the light. Still red. He craves a toothbrush. A shower, with a Karcher high–pressure cleaner. Then he'll scour the internet for plane tickets, make some quiet inquiries. Perhaps Cabrera y Machado hasn't yet replaced him.

Luis tries to pick details out of the cotton in his head. The dancing – salsa. Jesus. No other woman came close after that spectacle. Then, at the beach bar, Milena on the sand rolling up his pants. They walked under the moon and the fireworks until she stumbled, they both fell into the surf, came up drenched and sandy and laughing and – kissing. "We can dry off at my place," she said.

He knew, even through the haze of all that beer.

The traffic light blinks, turns orange. Did he miss the green? He steps on the clutch, the gearshift grates – anyone might think he's never driven a stick before. The Jeep lurches, catches, finally moves across the empty intersection.

Last night was a test, and he failed. Milena's found a weakness; she'll never trust him. No way he can work with her now, much less take over for her next year.

Something's off. Feels too simple.

In the three weeks he's known Milena (not counting the afternoon she interviewed him in Mexico five months ago), he's never seen her do anything, no matter how spontaneous it might seem, without calculating to the decimal every consequence, advantage, risk.

The self−pitying mini−him argues he's being paranoid. The Mexican gentleman in him is aghast at blaming the girl. But his gut feels the spot−on pang of truth. Last night wasn't just a test, wasn't just premeditated. It was blueprinted.

Luis marks a right turn, then a left. The *tck−tck−tck* sounds like his father's tongue clicking. You've been had, chamaco.

He pokes at the remote on the sun visor. The Warawara Resort gate swings open with a silent faltering, second−guessing itself. He shoves the gearshift into first, burns rubber shamelessly on the climb into the parking lot.

On the walkway to his condo, he fishes in a pocket for his keys with a chuckle of grudging respect. Ah, Milena. She owns him now. No wonder she looked so smug standing in her kitchen this morning, wearing his shirt. And he was so flustered, couldn't even find the words to ask for the shirt back. He fell for it, all of it. Well, she better enjoy her moment. He's taking the first flight out, cutting those puppet strings.

Where the hell are his keys? He clearly remembers them in his hand − when? Not today. Last night? Oh. At Milena's. He thought he was following her to *his* place, tried them on her front door until she giggled and handed him a Montblanc keyring. "Maybe this one?" It worked, and he pondered that for what felt like an instant but must've been longer because then he was falling on a wide bed and Milena was straddling him, undoing the remaining buttons of his shirt and whispering, "Luigi, I've been looking forward to this."

*Luigi.* And he felt like Rudolph Valentino while his self−esteem − and his keys − fell to the carpet, unnoticed.

There's a spare of the patio doors hidden in the bougainvillea by his pool. He cuts through the white−pebbled alley between his condo and the neighbor's, giant−steps up to the deck with knee creaking − and stops short.

There's a monster in the patio. Black, gigantic, sinister –
although this last tones down when the monster wags its tail.
*Thump–thumm–thumm–thump.*

Luis falls back to the pebbles. "Fuera. Shoo."

The monster opens its maw, rolls out a too–pink tongue.
Panting. Like a smile the Big Bad Wolf might give ol' Red
Riding Hood.

"Shoo. Go on." Luis claps loudly, but the only effect is a
speeding up of the tail. *Thumpathumpathumpa.*

He picks up a handful of pebbles. Damned if he's going to
let a dog manipulate him, too. But the monster's tail plunges
between his legs and he skits away with a very un–monster–ish
whimper before Luis lets fly the first stone. Black eyes, frightened
but also hurt, pine at Luis from across the pool. In the sun the
monster has become a skeleton: protruding hip bones, ribs so
marked Luis can count them – and the vertebrae above them.

Luis steps up to the deck. "Sorry, guy. I wouldn't've –"

The dog cowers, backs away, never takes his eyes off Luis.

"Look." Luis raises the hand with the pebbles, slowly, and
with a chalky clatter releases them to join their kin. "See? No
more rocks."

Is that a twitch at the tip of the tail?

"Forgive and forget, okay? I don't need a guilt trip."

The twitch this time is unmistakable.

Steps crunch in the alley. Vikram, Luis's Indian neighbor,
ducks into view from under the palm trees bordering his yard
and hollers, "Marjan, that dog is back!" Then he sees Luis. "Oh.
Hey, is that dog yours?"

Luis will never know what he would've said because Marjan,
Vikram's Dutch wife, calls out in her nasal whine from their
porch, "I'm calling Animal Control again."

"Wait."

Vikram looks Luis up and down. "It's yours then?"

Luis glances at the dog. He'll tell himself later the eyes did it.
In them he sees – imagines he sees – a plea. "That's right."

Vikram purses his mouth and studies the moment. "You need to take better care of him."

Great. Now he's a dog abuser.

But Vikram smiles before disappearing back into the palm trees. "I know a good vet," he says with a wave. "I'll get you the number."

Luis turns to the dog. "I just bought you some time, bud. Now scat."

The dog sits up and cocks an ear.

"You want to end up in the pound?" The dog shakes its head and Luis laughs. "Get outta here then."

But the dog stretches instead. The gesture looks ingratiating, almost flirtatious.

He's never owned a dog. Ma's allergies meant no pets. Later, living alone, he never had time. Not that he does now. Besides, he's leaving. Like, tomorrow.

Going back home, his own tail between his legs. Begging for his old job back. Giving Pa the satisfaction of another *I told you so*. They say decisions are choices between consequences. Compared to Pa, Milena is a beast he can tame. She might be surprised to find out how much he knows about puppeteering himself.

"You realize you'll need a bath, bud."

Tail wagging.

"Shots, too."

More tail wagging.

"Don't even know what you're agreeing to, do you?"

That panting wolf–smile.

"All right, then. Here, bud. Come on. You got to let me touch you."

# La Ronde / Madge and Gina

## by Townsend Walker

*That was it, that was it, it was all over for him, he hit me for the last time yesterday after his team lost the Orange Bowl in overtime and I'd said, honey, relax, chill out, it's only a game. Only a game he said, only a game, what the fuck do you know it's only a game. I don't know why I married such a dumb ass low−class broad. I must have been crazy thinking that you could ever learn anything and that snide remark you made to my mother on New Year's Eve about how the children never see me because I always come home after midnight, if I do come home. How do you think that makes me look in front of my own mother and father who never liked me anyway? You know what I'm going to do, I'm gonna shut you up good, you losing no good bitch. Take that you stupid slut, and that, and that. As long as you're into telling stories, I'll give you some to tell. You're going to tell everyone you slipped down the stairs New Year's Eve because you drank too much; you were too soused to walk. That's what you're going to tell people. You got that story? Good. Hasta la vista, baby.*

Gina and Madge are sitting in the Rose Club at the Plaza today.

"I lay on the floor for what must have been hours."

"Have you seen a doctor, Madge? You were always good at make-up, but you're hiding nothing from me. Your face is not good at all."

"I'll be okay, nothing broken and I didn't let him kick me in the stomach or back. Plus, I gave him a bloody nose, that's something."

"Waiter, two double martinis, Hendricks, please."

"Where were the kids while you were being Frank's punching bag?"

"Overnighting with school friends in the Village."

The women had been friends at Convent of the Sacred Heart in high school, two scholarship girls bonded against the snobs from the upper East Side; Gina was part of the tunnel crowd and Madge was from down on Avenue B. Scholarships to Barnard, majored in journalism, worked together on the *Post* and married well. Economically, if not otherwise for Madge. She'd bagged her blue blood, but it came with bruises. Gina married her second cousin Leo, a teddy bear and good father. His company had some luck and he got into doing construction for the state.

Other than the contrast afforded by hair and face – Madge, pale and blonde; Gina, olive and dark – they are sheathed by Herrera, shod by Blahnik and coated by mink. They shopped together, went to the matinees together and were working on a book, tentatively titled *If Only He Knew*. But never got their families together. Frank only associated with people who had blue eyes.

There is a couple in the corner they hadn't noticed earlier – older man, younger, much younger, woman sitting on a small plush sofa, holding hands. Brassy hair, lips much too red for her wan complexion, dress shiny and tight. She doesn't belong. He, on the other hand: silvery smooth hair, a recent tan (salon or tube), well-cut grey suit and solid pale blue tie. He looks uneasy. Like she insisted on coming to the Plaza to the point of no nookie and he's afraid of seeing someone he knows.

23

"See that tramp over there," Madge says. "That's the type Frank's been shacking up with."

"How do you know?"

"Dumb fuck had a photo on his phone."

"I think I've mentioned this before, like maybe 500 times, but why don't you divorce the bastard?"

"With all his money and friends, he'd make it hell for at least two years. And then I'd have to deal with him over the kids for another dozen. And there's those little you–know–whats his lawyer might uncover that would play havoc with the pre–nup. Plus little Olly, if he ever got around to a DNA sample."

"You mean the chastity belt clause? Why didn't you get one from him?"

"Marriage with Frank looked so good at the time, who was gonna quibble? Besides, he was the virgin when we met. Go figure."

Madge scoots her chair close to Gina's.

"Only way out is to put this guy away, for good. Way I figure is with Frank out of the way I'd have all of the money, not somewhere way south of half. He's a partner at Goldman, has a couple mil in stocks, plus a five million dollar life insurance policy. I could be a lot pickier next time around."

Gina crinkles her face. She's puzzled.

"You're gonna do what?"

"Not me, somebody. I need your help."

"This is a little out of my league."

"I thought you might know someone."

"Why do you think I'd know someone?"

"You're Italian, you're from Jersey, you'd know someone."

Gina sits back, twirls the liquor around her glass, sniffs it, holds it up to the light to see the yellowish color, sniffs it again and takes a long sip. She purses her lips as if she is about to say something, decides against it and looks over at the mismatched couple.

Madge is unsure what's going through her mind.

"Gina?"

"That was a stupid ass racist statement you made about Italians."

Madge lowers her head and turns bright red.

"Been with Frank too long. You're right about that remark, but I'm desperate."

"This is pretty serious stuff, you've thought about it? I mean, what would Sister Agnes say?"

They laugh.

"I'm thinking of the kids."

"Huh? Oh, if they had to spend time with Frank?"

"He is a total disaster as a father. Must be his upbringing, of which he had none. He takes them to the park, he loses them. One time we found Olly at the edge of the pond trying to pet the ducks."

"Well, I might know someone. My brother Joey."

Madge nods: she dated Joey when she was a sophomore.

"He sometimes runs with my uncle's crowd, who runs with, you know, those kind of people."

Madge jumps up and throws her arms around Gina to a symphony of clashing gold bracelets and dangling earrings.

"God, how I love you Gina."

"So what does Mr. Wonderful look like after all these years?"

"Not much changed from when you saw him ten years ago: six foot three, 200 pounds (going to chubby, he says it's Pilates' muscle), perpetually tanned (some gel he uses), curly black hair (going to gray, he says silver), still has that beak, Brooks Brother's dresser, loafers, always loafers with tassels. And those Hermes ties, you know, the silly patterned ones everyone on Wall Street wears. Outside, he's always got his Prada Aviators on, blue tint, all seasons."

"Waiter, a couple more please."

"Hey, you want to stay with me for a while 'til this cools off? Bring the kids; Leo will understand."

Friday, 3<sup>rd</sup> January 2014

# The Meet Cute

## by Derek Osborne

It has been quite a week. Usually the boat is down in the islands this time of year but a series of contracts is keeping them up in Miami. They're shooting two feature films and a *Miami Blue* episode. The *Miami Blue* crew, in particular, knows how to party. They are mostly young and single and ended up hanging out for the holidays.

Because New Year's Eve fell on a Tuesday the union people are having a field day. They've only been able to shoot a total of five days over the past fourteen. It's good for Max as well. Contractually, CBS has to hold the boat no matter what the reason. They had a good shoot the day before, going from 5AM right through sunset (the director wanted that wonderful pink light you only find in south Florida), so Max volunteered the boat for a little party this last evening by way of saying thanks. He figures a nice little gathering of twenty or so (most of the *Miami Blue* talent and senior staff have already flown out), some burgers and beer, a few guitars – a nice way to end the gig.

"Pam," he says into his SAT phone, it's his sister again, she's always calling at the worst possible times, "Pam, I'm in the middle of docking the boat."

"I don't care," she shoots back, "It's always something. Stop the engines and talk to me."

"I can't."

"Did you make the appointment?"

He hates these calls. Just when life is going well someone throws a glass of reality in his face.

"Yes," he says.

"When?"

"Later this month."

"What day?"

"I don't know, the 26^th I think."

Eddie, his first mate, is up by the bow giving hand signals. It's a big boat.

"Pam, I *really* have to pay attention to what I'm doing here."

"At Sloan−Kettering?"

"No," Max says, raising his voice, "Bob's fucking Cancer and Hot−Dog Emporium."

"Please don't yell." He can hear it, the tears coming. "I'm trying to help," his sister says.

He's trying to line things up so he doesn't take out the other guy's boat. He spins the big mahogany wheel, reverses the port engine and moves the joystick controlling the thruster. *Gadabout*, Max's boat, is a classic wooden sailing yacht, over ninety feet long including the bow sprit and mizzen brace. He and the crew are trying to squeeze in between two Italian Mega yachts there on the marina's main pier.

"I know you're trying to help," he says back into the phone.

"It's just bringing it all up again. I hate it."

"Pam, I'm fine."

The family is no stranger to cancer, if that is what's going on. His wife passed nearly six years before from ductal carcinoma, a three−year battle before that, a double mastectomy − the chemo − the waiting. Pam has a right to be worried, there's history on both sides of the family. Maybe it's been part of his own dance these past few months, maybe not. He's been feeling off, then fine, then off again for no reason. One thing they all learned from Maggie's death, early detection is key, and he's been avoiding.

"Hey, something to cheer you up," Max says, letting the boat slow to a stop, hovering there off the pier, "I'm falling in love with Rebecca Vasquez."

"Pia?" Pam says. Max can feel the shift; *Miami Blue* is her favorite show. "Is that who you're shooting with?"

"That's one of them."

"Why didn't you tell me? You met her? What's she like? What's Thaddeus like?"

"Pam, I'm docking the god damn boat. I'll tell you when I come for the tests."

He can see Eddie with a *what—the—fuck* look on his face. Eddie came with the boat. He's Jamaican and has all their easy ways but he's also a serious waterman. Over the years he's become a good friend.

"Get their autographs?" Max can hear Pam saying over the phone.

"Goodbye, Pam."

"Please?"

"Love you …"

"Don't blow this off …" she starts, but he's already shut it down. He's promised them all he'll go for the tests. His sister's no dummy, she got his daughters involved. He's had calls from all three.

Moving the thruster again, he and Eddie start slipping the yacht toward the pier. No words are needed; they've done it a thousand times. Eddie stands ready to throw the lines.

Max is doing his best not to look at the gathering crowd. It's not that he can't dock the boat and talk on the phone at the same time, that's a piece of cake; it's the other thing, the rumor that Rebecca Vasquez, the actress who plays Pia on *Miami Blue*, intends on joining the party. Seems she has family in Miami and has been staying there during the shoot. Seems her personal assistant, Anja, has hit it off with Eddie. Seems Anja and Rebecca like to hang out together. He's ignoring the other thing, what Anja told Eddie, that her boss thinks Max is "interesting." Max has been in the business long enough to know the flirting that often goes on is just a part of the show. Everyone flirts; everyone's *on*, it's in their blood. It reminds him of what Katharine Hepburn once told a reporter when asked what made her a star. "I don't know," she said, "but whatever it is, I've got it." They all have it to some degree, some more than others; Rebecca, a lot more than others. There's no denying Max is attracted, who wouldn't be, but there's also a pragmatic side that allows him to skipper a big boat across oceans, run a successful business, deal with producers whose sole job is to get the most bang for the studio's buck. Life holds fewer illusions these days, especially since his wife's passing.

But Max has been letting himself fall more and more into the fantasy. It's fun. They haven't actually spoken; just the stolen glances and study–hall notes from Anja to Eddie. He's feeling it though, that tingle, that mutual vibration, slipping past her there on the boat, both of them consummate professionals, avoiding eye contact, and yet. Her wanting to come to the party doesn't prove anything, no more than she enjoys her co–workers and likes the boat, and everyone loves *Gadabout*, so much he always assumes it's the boat and not its skipper they want to be with. *She's half your age*, he reminds himself, working the thrusters while minding the stern. Once upon a time he might have laid siege to her doorstep. In truth, he's feeling more like fifteen than fifty–five, replaying each moment, dissecting every nuance, especially after what Anja said the night before, study–hall be damned.

"That's not all she's going to miss."

The conversation had been about the boat, or so he thought. He'd gone out for a bite to eat with her and Eddie.

"Becky wanted to come out with us tonight but, you know, appearances and all that."

"Of course," Max said.

29

"Don't misunderstand," Anja went on, "Beck could care less. But there's paparazzo down here." And then she had leaned in, and this is what had him looped in the loops of her hair, "I think she'd really like a tour of the boat."

Standing now at the helm, working the thruster, he steals a moment to look at the dock. There have to be fifty people bunched up like kids on a class trip, but there near the center, a bit off right, as if they've framed and lit the scene to bring out her eyes and that wild hair she prefers off camera, the V—neck tee, her pirate's smile, Rebecca has indeed shown up. He knows that smile; right about then a fait accompli, no use trying to hide anymore. It went like that, right then, right there, from doubt to surrender. The very best, Max thinks – the very best – he'll have a nice memory of a divine two—week flirtation, the rising star and the middle—aged sea captain, another day in the life.

"Calm down," he says beneath the engine's monotone, drinking in that look aimed right at him.

"Max!"

It's Eddie again; he's shouting and pointing, their bowsprit ready to spear the other boat's canopy. Max reverses just in time. Eddie raises his hands in the air, again. Max works the lever and the boat backs out a few meters. He steals another look at the dock. The crowd seems oblivious but she hasn't missed a thing. It both embarrasses and makes him like her all the more, every inch of her laughing now, a good—natured, sly little grin spreading fast across her face.

*Gotcha,* her eyes are saying.

Max throws a line to one of the marina's attendants and shuts down the engines. The men on the pier start hauling the yacht alongside.

*Yes,* he's thinking, returning her smile, *you have indeed.* He lets his own smile fade, holding her there. *You're not the only one who's got it,* he's telling her. She blushes – looks down – comes back radiant as ever. He's feeling quite proud of himself when a return line thrown from the dock smacks him right in the face. The crowd doubles over. He grabs the line using every ounce of self—restraint. Even Eddie is holding onto himself, doing his best to look the other way. But Rebecca isn't laughing, far from it. He sees her there, the crowd fading and laughter blending out into the evening – her smile – the one he was sure he would never see again.

*Sweet Jesus,* he's thinking, *what do I do now?*

Saturday, 4th January 2014

# Ralph Rudinsky here …

## by Gloria Garfunkel

Ralph Rudinsky here Chief of Quality Assurance for a large diversified corporation Orwellian Industries a big important job that's hard to keep up with so it's already January 4 and I still haven't made my New Year's Resolutions because I have so much to do I even take work home so I feel it's OK for me to take these few minutes out of my hectic work for resolutions now which include being perfect at all times not let my bipolar disorder interfere with my work though I am in a manic episode now and hypergraphic writing and and hyperverbal and do not want to obsess about my boss Stan Stealth cat fur grain moths my manipulative Borderline Personality secretary Serena or my passive−aggressive assistant Jake or my sociopathic boss did I mention him and be nice to everyone especially people I hate as mentioned above and just yes Stan to death and get a lot of work done which is easy in a manic episode because I never sleep and can make up for the depressive crashes when I can live on Ritalin−Sudafed and caffeine and still cannot stay awake and never tell anyone outside my family and girlfriend Chloe that I'm bipolar or they'll hold it against me like they did at my last job when I was fired.

# Carmine

## by John Wentworth Chapin

Pinks and oranges plume outward in a gaudy riot, each burgundy— or lavender—accented petal evoking Mardi Gras or day—glo psychedelia. It overshadows the carefully crafted competition: pure creamy yellow, black and white bull's eye, Kermit's head. It's supposed to be a flower, but it's more like Barbie's Malibu Dream House: Tornado Aftermath. Nothing holds a candle to this most glorious of cupcakes. Charles tells the woman behind the counter that he wants the pink and orange flower, and she nods, carefully boxing it for him.

"It's for a celebration," he prompts. She doesn't respond, and he wonders if she slams closed all doors to conversation at home or just at work.

Charles has always been a celebrator of anniversaries, milestones, rites of passage. ♡JUSTIN♡ *Happy three months of dating! Thank you so much, Mrs. Blaisdell: I have simply loved the first half of ninth grade. DARRELL — Congratulations on 27 months of sobriety, Mister Straight Arrow!!!!* There were made—to—order t—shirts, celebratory emails strewn with clip art, baked goods. There was champagne (though not for Darrell).

As he reaches into one pocket to pay for the cupcake, another pocket vibrates, followed by the opening notes of *Everything's Coming Up Roses*. The bakery woman seems deaf to the music, as though classic showtunes regularly leap from her customers' persons.

"It's my mother," he explains. "Everyone deserves a custom ringtone."

He wishes she would say something arch, like *Your mother? I thought Ethel Merman was in your pants.* She doesn't, however. The witty repartee in Charles's life comes from his own mouth, frequently in hindsight.

He answers his phone with an apologetic grin to the bakery woman. His mother launches into a story about rubbery shrimp scampi. He listens a moment, and the bakery woman hands him his change. If he takes the change, she will disappear into bowls of frosting or *mille–feuilles.* He's not ready to give up on her yet.

Charles interrupts. "Did you call to celebrate?"

She and the bakery woman are both silent.

Charles says, "It's been one whole month since December 5."

The bakery woman rattles out her change–holding hand; his mother at least has the social skills to ask for clarification.

"That was the day of the *accident,*" he says. The bakery woman leaves the change resting on the glass counter, tapping it and nodding at him. "I'm trying not to remember all the blood," he says loudly. "I'm celebrating that I am alive!" The bakery woman retreats to a tray of cookies.

Charles's mother makes a few unsatisfactory noises; she doesn't want him dwelling on the macabre, but she does want him dwelling on the shrimp scampi. He begs off with an excuse that he is at the register at a bakery, as though his attention were required. He promises to call her later, which he will remember tomorrow that he did not do.

He collects his change and the cupcake and calls his thanks to the woman across the store. He wishes she'd tell him a story about when her sister got diagnosed with Stage II cervical cancer but last November they celebrated her victory of five years of remission.

She doesn't.


At home, he sets the cupcake on a plate. Outrageous colors. He's even more delighted by it now than he was earlier. He doesn't want to eat it and ruin it; it will be dry, because it's way too beautiful to taste good. He lets it be and tries to find a distraction.

He flips open his laptop, but he just doesn't feel like working this afternoon. He steals a glance at the cupcake. One month! He calls his friend Stephanie, but she doesn't answer. He texts his friend Jeff, but Jeff doesn't answer. That his pool of friends is so shallow worries Charles.

He has an epiphany: no one is answering because he's dead. He's not alive – he died in the accident, and now he's a wandering ghost.

This unnerves him, and he seeks solace in the cupcake, a candied bonfire in his slate−colored kitchen. Wandering ghosts don't have day−glo cupcakes. Just to be sure, he cuts a wedge and pops a bite into his mouth. It's surprisingly moist and tasty, and the riotous frosting is softer than he expected. Orange, with a hint of pomegranate.

"You are alive, and that is one damn good cupcake, Charles," he announces to his empty apartment. It's meant to be jovial and nerve−settling, but his voice bounces off the walls.

He abandons his cupcake, and the apartment door slams behind him.


Charles climbed out of his car, sidestepping a city lamppost, then jerked his head toward a loud, awful crash of metal and glass. A runaway Volkswagen tore into the sides of two cars and continued at full speed down the sidewalk toward him. It hit a woman. She flew onto the windshield in a spray of blood. Two boys turned to see the gray Volkswagen; Charles couldn't see their faces but he saw them both killed, one tossed onto the hood, the other crumpled under the tires. The car continued straight at Charles and rammed into his car, the lamppost, and a mailbox, all at once. The woman and the boy on the hood flew forward onto Charles as the car came to a complete, hissing stop. Five seconds of mayhem ended with three people dead and Charles standing on a city sidewalk covered in crimson gore, shocked into a stupor but otherwise entirely unharmed.

He looked around him; a heavyset woman stepped out of a sandwich shop, her mouth open, looking straight at Charles.

"That car was headed right for you. If ..." she mouthed, before she started screaming.

If his car door hadn't been open. If the lamppost hadn't been right there. If if if. Charles saw death coming at him and he didn't even get out of the way: death just stopped.


Charles is entirely a−religious. It makes no sense to him that he was spared for a reason. Charles doesn't feel guilty.

"I feel lucky," he tells the group of four guys clustered at the bar. Charles has bought everyone in this group a round, and they have twice returned the favor. They are a familiar bunch, but he knows none of them before tonight. One guy − Charles thinks his name is Tony, but that seems wrong − asks what's changed since the accident.

"I feel like I got a new start," he says.

"Doing what?" Maybe−Tony asks.

Charles doesn't have an answer. Something about the guy unsettles him. In a good way. "I usually have a bunch of New Year's resolutions," he says. "Not this year."

"Do you love your job?" Maybe–Tony asks. Charles does PR for a printing company; it's all old guys who complain about Twitter and the death of print and they think it's a riot that Charles is gay and drill him with inappropriate questions.

Charles shakes his head.

"Did you think about quitting, chasing a passion?"

Charles smiles. "I almost got killed. I didn't win the lottery."

Maybe–Tony says, "Sounds like maybe you got a wake–up call and went back to sleep."

*Now that's some witty repartee*, Charles thinks.



"That is one out–of–control confection," Maybe–Tony says when Charles ushers him into his kitchen. They were making out in the front hall a moment ago, vodka and lust.

Charles offers him a bite.

"Are you asking me to split your cupcake?" Maybe–Tony snickers.

"You told me to chase a passion," Charles says.

They set the cupcake between them on the couch and nibble at it. The conversation rapidly abandons flirtation.

Maybe–Tony says, "Most people would get very religious right about now, thanking God and carrying on." Charles confesses disinterest in religion and confides to Maybe–Tony his weird moment earlier when he thought he was a ghost.

"Not that I believe in ghosts," Charles says quickly, and then he resumes his story.

While Maybe–Tony listens, he haphazardly traces a bright pink scar on his jaw, as though he's tickling himself or reassuring himself that his scar is still there. It's oddly compelling, making Charles want to touch it. The longer Charles talks with Maybe–Tony, the less he wants to get naked. His desire is to stay up all night talking.

So Charles does something entirely unexpected for Charles: he tells Maybe–Tony his desire.

Maybe–Tony breaks apart the final piece of cupcake and tells about the time he fell off a chairlift. Charles licks the last of the bright orange frosting from his fingers.

# First Impression

## by Lynn Beighley

"Jenn, you'll sit here," Bill says, putting his hand on the back of the chair next to his. Because I don't know these people very well yet, I obey. If this wasn't my second week at my new job, and my first time out for lunch with my new coworkers, I still would have obeyed, because I'm like that. My seat is in a corner. To my left is Bill, to my right is a dusty windowsill where two flies are having sex. I've never seen copulating flies before, but there's no mistaking it.

I've learned that Bill has a big announcement to make, and apparently any excuse to go out to lunch is generally a good one. Bill has escorted a group of seven of us to Kontry Jed's All U Kin Et Buffet. We're waiting for the waitress to take our drink orders. "I bring my grandmother here almost every Sunday. They know me," he says. "I'm a regular, and they treat me well because they know they'll get a ten percent tip from me, every time."

I look around at the other customers, clearly also regulars. Ten percent sounds cheap to me, but I suspect that at this particular establishment it's on the high end of the tipping spectrum.

None of us has ever been to Kontry Jed's. Bill stands up, as though he's going to give a speech. Which he does. "Since it's all you can eat," Bill explains to the table, "you should be strategic. Start with the expensive foods, like the meats, not the cheap starches. Don't fill up on the bread." His intensity embarrasses me. I see a few people snickering.

I hear one of my new coworkers, I don't remember his name, whispering to his neighbor in his best Bill voice, "No, don't fill up on the bread! No bread, it's not strategic." I don't think Bill heard, he's paying rapt attention to the drink orders being taken by a dead-eyed waitress in a stained, wrinkled white shirt. But I heard, and Noname has earned a place on my asshole list.

The buffet is, well, let's just say that I hate buffets, and this place epitomizes why. I think the horny flies' offspring will find a welcoming home in the macaroni and cheese. I stick to the salad bar. Figuratively, although if I touched the gloppy counter, it might be literally.

"Of course he wants to sit next to you. Our Bulldozer likes redheads," my new coworker Alan whispers to me as we fill our plates. I've already learned that Bill Plover has a nickname he doesn't know about, Bulldozer, or more often shortened to Bull when his coworkers are joking about him. It's partly because he's a little on the short side, with a thick frame. You wouldn't call him fat, just very bulky. Bulky Bull Plover.

Bill plods as he cases the food stations. He moves like a stegosaurus on his stocky legs, which doesn't lessen his resemblance to construction equipment.

"But it's not just how he looks," my boss Jonathan told me in an unguarded moment in his office. "It's not only the way Bulldozer moves. It's also that he's so on and off. Black and white. Hit or miss. He has no low gears. He plows through things as if they aren't there. If a bulldozer was a human, he'd be our Bully boy." He pauses and adds, urgently, "Hot and cold. That's it." I didn't know how to respond to such frank talk about a coworker. Was this some kind of test to see if I gossip? I just nodded and the conversation shifted to more appropriate, but less interesting topics, like ordering office supplies and reserving conference rooms.

We're all finally back at the table, me with my wilted iceberg salad and iced tea. The flies are gone. Bill stands and starts tapping his water glass with his knife. I watch it nearly topple, and grab it before it does, getting a sharp rap to my knuckles from Bill's knife.

"Here's my news," Bill says, glancing at everyone, but mostly gazing at me, "I've been selected to be on a reality television show." He sits down as everyone starts asking questions. We're sitting close enough together that I can feel his body heat.

Bulldozer on *Survivor*? Surely not. *Amazing Race*? *Biggest Loser*? No, none of the current crop of reality TV shows I can think of makes sense for him. But he's going to be on television, and that impresses me, even though I hate that it does.

"It's a new show called *You Tell Me*," he explains. "It's about crowdsourcing. About the hive mind. For the next year or so, social media will tell me what to do. Little things like what I should wear, but also bigger things, like dating decisions."

Everyone looks at me, I'm not imagining this.

# Wingy

## by Andrew Stancek

I fly.

That is the blunt truth with which it all begins. It is as good an opening as *In the beginning was the Word and the Word was with God and the Word was God.*

I have no motor. I have no Atlas−like musculature, special body parts or contraption of any sort. I don't chant incantations, turn keys, push buttons. I don't have an IQ of 200 or more. I am as ordinary as most of the six billion inhabitants of this planet and I have, for the first time in the history of mankind, figured out what birds do instinctively.

I fly.

I am not imagining it. No reason to lock me up. Experts of a thousand kinds have seen and tested and the whole Internet world has oohed and aahed and it cannot be explained away.

I fly.

My name is Adam. In retrospect it's funny, prescient, ironic. It's a name given to me by my parents who meant nothing by it. They were not harking back to the first man, formed out of clay by the Almighty's hand. They chose a name they were familiar and comfortable with, one in my father's family for generations.

Zajac, my last name, well, all the hilarity you can have with that. I've heard it throughout my childhood, my normal childhood before The Event, and since the millions of words written about me, I've heard a lot more. My parents are Slovak and the name means rabbit, or more precisely hare. Yes, the headlines made it into Bunny, told me to hear, hear, to come here and there and everywhere. Adam Zajac, A to Z, is significant as well; I am of course the alpha and the omega. The first ever and after me, perhaps, the deluge. In North America the name came to be pronounced the English way, so in my teenage years the wits called out "Hey, Jack." Enormously clever.

What else needs to be said? I already said I am unexceptional. Or was, anyway. I am not, truly am not, comparing myself in any way to Einstein but I've always liked that line of his, "I have no special talent. I am only passionately curious." That describes me as well. In addition to the curiosity, I had the great fortune to be ill and bed–ridden for almost two years. During that time I was able to read, to think, to observe, to truly observe. I have imagination, curiosity, observational talent, and I was given leisure. I could indulge in ways of thinking that in an adult would be laughed at. Professors of aerodynamics, engineers of all sorts, they have prestige to think of, deadlines, adult preoccupations, but to me those did not apply. Leonardo was of course the greatest of all time, but his mind took him all over the place. He was not ordinary; he was a genius, and that is what prevented him from pursuing one idea to its fruition – he had thousands. I was ordinary and only had one. And I did it.

I fly.

I've grown to accept the name they hung on me: Wingy. It sounds like loopy, dingbatty, wacky. They didn't really mean that. If you pushed them, they would chuckle and say I am nuts, of course. I am one of a kind. No one has ever done what I do every day, routinely. I've shown it hundreds of times and they cannot prove I am a fake or a charlatan. So they admire me but resent me as well. Wingy is descriptive. A headline writer used it first and it stuck. My feats, including the name, have gone viral.

And as I said, I am fine with it. Wingy. If you want, you can hear other words in there, too: king, ring, sing, longing.

I've decided to write my story, my side. So much has been written about me that you might think another word isn't needed. Of course I cooperated at the beginning, with everyone: the scientists, the doctors, the engineers, the writers and the hyenas. I got sick of it, and I became less open. I'm no fool. I know many would prefer I was never born, never came to the world's attention. But they cannot undo me.

Maybe no one will ever read this. I'm not writing for a learned journal or for the popular press, only for me. Maybe it'll be read next week and maybe a hundred years from now. So I'll pour out the me whom no one knows, my feelings, my way. If you know the story, move on, skip a part or two. But I just may surprise you. Even if you think you know, something may startle. Hold onto your seats and enjoy the ride.

Wednesday, 8th January 2014

# Isa

## by Rachel Ambrose

Isa, my roommate, is a great snack buyer, so I almost never go
hungry even though I hate the grocery store. Maybe if my
apartment wasn't so comfortable, I would feel the need to leave
it unprompted once in a while. But that day is not today.

I do leave my apartment to go to work for an elderly lawyer
named Mrs. Hatfield who smells like lavender soap and lilies. I
tidy her desk, empty the trash, answer her phone and schedule
her calendar. Every so often someone comes in to see her and I
escort them to her office, where she greets them with a powdery
kiss on the cheek and an offer of gumdrops. I have a little plaque
on my desk with 'Claire Worthington, Administrative Assistant'
written on it. My pay could be called meager at best. I pay my
bills, but paying for anything else is pretty impossible. But then
Saturday mornings hit, and isn't that the best, logging on to your
bank account page and seeing two or three hundred more dollars
in there, like the money fairies have visited during the night? I
pay off my bills straightaway and then look at the double-digit
amount that's left, and I think about buying truffled fries or
imported tea from England or an eggplant-colored cape. I
always talk myself out of it, but Saturday mornings are precious,
dream-laced things nonetheless.

I would like to burrow into my little yellow pool of shag rug
and stay there, like a little mouse, sometimes poking my nose out

for bits of cheese and fruit. The sun shines on it every day and I think it would be a lovely way to spend my time, all huddled up in warmth and gold.

Worryingly, these days, it seems like my hermitting issues are moving to take over, well, my entire life. Or rather, they're making me avoid actually existing. Well, I'm alive. Of course I am. I eat and breathe. But getting out there with people, interacting, behaving like a real adult of twenty–six years, that's been much harder these days. My therapist, a softspoken Irish lady named Ruthie, has suggested I keep a journal. "Being accountable, if only to yourself for your own experiences, will light a fire under your ass," she told me at our last session. Ruthie has a gift for the well–placed curse. In this case, it surprises me so much that I immediately go out, buy a composition notebook, and start writing down words with which to further berate myself. Somehow I don't think that this is what Ruthie had in mind.

But, see, somewhere after college, or maybe right before it ended, the fire under my ass just went out. The constant striving to be the best, to hand in papers well before deadline, to rewrite those papers three or four times the night before they were due, all that passion, just left in a big hurry. "Graduate college!" your parents tell you. "Go get a job and live your life!" Well, plonk, here I am. I've graduated college. I've got a job. What do you want me to do now, authority figures? Give me a map, because without all those demanding voices in my head, I'm a little bit lost. "Be more ambitious!" my parents tell me now. "Ask that old dingbat for a raise! Ask for more responsibilities! Freshen up your resumé." But I don't HAVE to do that. I'm feeding myself. I'm paying my little portion of the rent. My cell phone is still connected. So it's a shift from things I felt I was bound to do, to things I feel I might or could do. I could, if my little heart so chose, ask Mrs. Hatfield for a raise. I could ask for more responsibilities. I might even be able to get a new job if I tried hard enough. But the thing is, I'm utterly satisfied with the modicum of responsibilities I have. I see Isa bring home these stacks of papers from her office every day, and granted, it pays more than mine, but I might just like sitting on my couch with my laptop and Netflix and takeout Chinese. Or at least I think I like it. How do you know if you like something new if it isn't shoved in your face? If no parent or teacher is putting it on a spoon and making airplane noises until it gets close enough to your mouth that you have to open up your lips and try it? What, you mean you people just go out there and give it a shot? Who are you? How did you get that way? Tell me.

You know that if you switch around the letters in 'tried', you get 'tired'? Maybe you get tired after you've tried too hard. I think that's what happened to me. Not even tired as in "I'm tired, I need a nap." I mean tired like that old faded blue sofa in your den that's slowly become covered with stuff, so much stuff that you can't even see it anymore, and it's not a proper sofa. But even though it's tired, and not really serving its purpose in life, it's still sitting there in your den, and you're used to seeing it there, and the familiarity of it soothes you enough that you don't want to go get a new one.

So it's a bit of a shock when Isa comes home one night with a nip on her face and a cloud over her head. She gets angry easily, she's constantly blaming it on her Mexican and Spanish heritage, but tonight she's really pissed. I corner her after she's taken a shower and is wrapping her hair up in a topknot on her head. "Hey, what's going on with you? Bee in your bonnet?"

"More like a nest of wasps," she says, tossing her head. "You remember how my little brother Paulo slipped on the ice a month ago and hit his head? I guess he has to have someone move in full time to take care of him and drive him to doctors' appointments, so my parents picked me to be the nursemaid."

"Why can't they do it?" I ask, irritated for her.

"You know my mom and dad," she says. "She's always off on some hippie retreat, he's busy with his engineering firm. How dare I expect my parents to parent, eh?"

"Well ..." I say. "Is it going to be for long? How many doctors' appointments can he go to?"

"They don't know how long it's going to take," says Isa. "If I were you, I'd try and find a new roommate. I don't want you having to pay all the rent all the time, I know you can't afford it. Want me to put an ad on Craigslist and see if I can find anyone who's not a crazy axe murderer before I go?"

"Sure, thanks," I say, relieved that she's taking point on this; what in the world would I say? 'Part Time Hermit Seeks Someone Who Will Buy Potato Chips and Pay Rent'? 'Part Time Hermit Wants Someone Silent to Live with Her'? Right.

"Maybe I can come see you on weekends," I say. "We can work out a rota or something if you need help. How many doctor's appointments can one person possibly have?"

"Yeah," says Isa. "They want me over there in a few days, though, so I've gotta start packing now. Wanna come help?"

I snort. "Please. Let me just sit here in my misery and mope for a while about your untimely departure from our hitherto blissful living situation. You don't know, I might get someone who doesn't wash and uses his dirty boxers as dish rags."

"Sweetie, you know me better than that," soothes Isa. "I'll find you someone nice. Nachos for supper later?"

Nachos sound good, but I would have traded all the queso in the world for her to never grab her suitcase from the closet.

# Carpet Muncher

## by Gill Hoffs

I have a double–bed at home, and I have a side I like to sleep on, but what the latter is depends on who is paying for my company that night. I wake up on the left today in a rented bed, next to Robin, whose wife understands him well enough but doesn't have the figure or temperament to stand beside him at a business do and impress the other suits with Robin's good taste, or the stamina to help him blow off steam with a half–hour blowjob afterwards. Apparently it makes her jaw ache and her cheeks sore, and he has a tendency to get some in her eye. Now I've known him a while, I'm sure his aim was deliberate.

When he was interviewing me at the agency, he said, "I'm wondering about your oral endurance," as he drummed his fingertips on the arm of the chair, eying my lips with an air of scepticism.

I raised an eyebrow at him, plucked the office boy's vanilla thickshake from his desk, and sucked the cup dry, holding my potential client's gaze all the while. I prefer to avoid super–sweet icecream drinks – I'm a coffee girl, myself – but it was worth the calories to snag Robin. I could smell the top–notes of his aftershave and knew it cost more than Cristal.

Once we'd agreed on our first 'date', and I'd kissed both cheeks goodbye in the London way, which seemed posh for Manchester and no doubt impressed him with my professionalism, we fell into a routine of coffee and catchup, dinner with colleagues from overseas, then the blowjob before bed. He likes to wake up with me in the morning. I don't feel I'm really earning my overnight fee by just spooning with him, tucking the duvet around his feet when it's cold, and serving him espresso in my special way before he returns to work ... but I can live with it.

This morning it's dark when he finally murmurs "Fuck" and knocks his Blackberry to the floor, silencing the beeeeeep of the alarm. I've already laid out his shirt and tie the way he likes them, smooth and flat and formal on my side of the bed, with his trousers hanging off the chair nearby, and fresh socks on my pillow. Years of working early shifts in a supermarket, stacking tins on shelves and indulging my OCD through 'facing' the labels just so, means I rarely sleep past 5.30 anyway. I've had plenty of time to shower then prep his hotel room using just the streetlight reflecting up from the city streets below and call down to room service, as well as email my gran thanks for the Christmas present of potpourri and plan Friday and the working weekend that lies ahead.

Robin rolls onto his back, angles his arms in triangles as he tucks his hands behind his head, and waits for the knock at the door. The threads of blood lacing the whites of his eyes make his blue eyes seem all the more vivid, and I can see from the tepee over his crotch where the rest of the spare blood in his body has gone. I smile at him, and make a show of stretching across the table by the window to tweak the curtains back, then saunter across the thick red carpet to flick the little brass knob beside the doorframe, turning the side lights on, and, from the groan in the bed, Robin too.

We're several floors up, twenty maybe, and the top floor of an office is opposite our room. Its windows glow yellow and I can see some poor wretch on the phone there already as the cleaners drag a vacuum around by the hose like a reluctant child. Robin, for all his tasteful clothes and business−like exterior, loves me to put on a show. I sometimes think he should have been a film director.

The knock comes, and I raise an eyebrow at Robin, who licks his lips, nodding for me to open it, and I do. Naked.

The guy holding the coffee must be used to it by now. I half expect him to comment on the winter weight I gained from too many (working) Christmas dinners, or the too-long pubes I had my stylist wax into the silhouette of a Christmas tree (I even wore a crystal stick-on star for the man I had dinner with on Christmas Eve, but it's long gone now, tucked into his wallet as a reminder of services rendered) which reminds me, I need to go get that seen to before tonight's appointment with Tony the Tongue. But no. Just a smirk, then theatrically raised eyebrows and a gasp of morning breath. He pauses, tray in hand, letting his eyes wander to my tits.

I step back into the room, allowing him to step forward, and without a word, I take the little white cup of coffee from the tray. And stumble, on purpose, so the rich black fluid slops a few drops over the side. They hit the carpet, not my foot – when Robin first told me what he wanted, I practised at home until I could spill it just right – and the waiter finally speaks.

"Well, that was careless. Don't expect me to clean it up."

Not quite the script we'd worked through earlier, but close enough. I wink at him, and put the coffee down on the little table at the end of the bed, where Robin watches from the pillow, pupils like LPs blacking out the blue.

Now the icky bit.

Bending over, I place my hands on the plush red carpet, wiggling my arse a little at the coffee guy, then get down on my knees, lower my head, and make Robin think I'm sucking the stain out. I make slurping noises with my mouth, like when I suck his cock, and make sure my legs are just far enough apart for the floor show. My hair is long enough to hide my face, and by biting my lips a bit and sucking them in through my teeth a few times, I can make them swell and redden enough to give

Robin the impression I've delivered the show he's looking for. When I hear Robin's breathing quicken I discreetly tap my toes. As I moan and wriggle my arse a little faster, the room service guy takes his cue.

"Have you cleaned my carpet?"

I sit up, nod, and as I slo−o−o−owly lick my lips and sigh, and he squints at the wet patch on the floor, we hear the mnngh from my client on the bed. Ignoring the mess now dampening the sheets, the coffee guy purses his lips, and leaves.

The door closes and, getting up off my knees, I take Robin the rest of his espresso in bed. He tosses it back in one gulp, and hands me the empty cup with a stubble−cheeked smile before crumpling the sheets to the side. Swinging his hairy legs off the bed, he stands up with his cock bobbing like a nodding dog in the back of a minicab, and pads through to the shower.

I step into my day outfit of green knitted dress and warm−but−still−sexy boots, smear cherry balm across my lips, pick up my bag from the table by the bed and close the door behind me as I step into the hall.

The lift doors open, and I walk into the wood−panelled elevator and press L, daydreaming about the hours ahead. Time for a browse round the sales before I take the tram home, and feed the cat before I meet tonight's client.

And a wax.

Tony might not mind a mouthful of bush, but I'm pretty sure he'd gag at a Christmas tree.

Friday, 10<sup>th</sup> January 2014

# Snakes and Snails

## by Susan Tepper

They keep the schoolyard under lock and key. It's silly. Teachers all over the place and those aides who don't know nothing but stand around, anyhow, like guards.

I move my car from spot to spot. It's better that way. Today being Friday is the last day I get to see the kids. Weekends are dull. I'm parked under a big leafless tree across from the chain link fence they put up to protect the kids. The kids, squealing and screaming, are such little darlings. I call them *my little darlings*. They can't hear me saying this, of course, being that I'm in the car and they're in the school yard.

Each week I pick my two favorites. Two favorite little darlings. On Monday I first picked the red head boy who I would guess to be about seven years old, based on the sizes of the other kids, tho' my red head boy is taller and thinner than most of them. He has spirit! I love a kid with spirit.

I had spirit growing up until my da beat the crap of it. Beat it with a belt. Not a good thing to do to a boy. You turn off a boy's natural spirit, you get a crouching, fearful bag o' bones. That's what you turn your boy into from the beatings. They said I failed in school because I was *slow*. They didn't get it that I had to move slow, always slow, to avoid pissing off the old man. You pissed that bastard off, the belt came out faster than a boy can stick out his tongue.

My car has a fair amount of acorn dings from sitting under these big trees during the fall. I would hear those acorns smacking the hood and the roof and there wasn't a thing I could do. If I moved the car, chances were pretty good I wouldn't be able to find another parking spot. It's crowded around here from the apartment houses. Too many cars and not enough good spots from where I can watch the kids.

Last week a cop car drove real slow past me and went around the loop and drove past me again. I took out the newspaper I save for emergencies. I put it against the steering wheel and read an article about the rise and fall of cholesterol among Chinese peasants. I read every word so carefully I can still practically recite it by heart. Goes to show.

The red head boy is very good on the jungle gym. These days they cover the ground with thick black rubber to protect the kids who fall. The read head kid never falls and he pulls some pretty tricky stunts. He can twist into a pretzel then swing to another bar.

Not to leave out my other favorite for the week: a small kid with blond hair. Towheads they call them. He's a fearful little tyke, the kind you want to cradle on your lap and rock. Back and forth, back and forth, back and forth. Whispering in his little ear that there is nothing in the world to be afraid of in my arms on my lap.

I want to get out of the car and stretch my legs but this is impossible. My one leg aches from being snarled under the steering wheel. This piece of shit car is older than dirt. I really need to buy a new one, something in a good color that will blend. A taupe color or a dark tan. Those cars people never remember. They get into accidents, hit and runs, and no witness can quite finger them. For the time being I'm stuck with this old Dodge Dart. A blue, much too bright. I'm sure it's what caught that cop's attention. But, cops being cops, he did his round and probably went off to do a drug deal or visit a prostitute. Those cops don't fool anyone who grew up in a neighborhood like this one.

My little blondie boy is playing in the dirt with a pail. He's kneeling and digging. One of the teacher aides is talking to him (I can only imagine) and now he's getting to his feet, dragging his little self toward the swings. She must've told him to be more physical. My da used to throw that shit at us kids: be more physical. "OK, Da, right."

Somehow that gets me to laughing. I was in Desert Storm when he shut his eyes for the last time. Now that was a trip. Desert Storm *and* the old man's sudden ending. *If I have to go make it quick*, he used to say.

"Well bless you, Da, bless you." What would make him think he was different from the rest of us? "We all gotta go, Da." It busts me up laughing again saying this stuff.

Now my little red head boy is chucking handfuls of shit at some other kids. Everything they do just drives me up a wall! I want to grab them and spin them around and tickle them until they fall down on the ground the spittle dripping off their chins from so much fun and laughter! *Snakes and snails and puppy dog tails, that's what little boys are made of.*

Saturday, 11<sup>th</sup> January 2014

# Father Eleanor

## by Jessica McHugh

Father Edward McKenzie powders his nose, pretending the Almay in the vintage Duska tin is authentic. His grandmother's old phonograph sits quiet in the corner, but as he sways to Kay Starr crooning from his laptop, he imagines her song floats from the player instead. It's a harder stretch than the makeup, but it's easier to believe than the delusions about his wardrobe. As much as he imagines his body hugged by mocha lace and fur trim, the mirror betrays his fantasies. His 'gown' is no more than an ill-fitting bathrobe torn to the thigh. But he has time before he's forced to face reality. Tossing a blanket over the mirror, Edward feels beautiful again.

He pictures gloved hands beckoning him into a waltz. There's no chance he'll refuse. Even when secondhand heels constrict his feet, crushing his toes to a feminine taper, he is more beautiful for the pain. In the muscular arms of his waltzing partner, he is as dainty as the January snow grazing his window. He doesn't care who his partner is, only that he has someone who won't shrink back from his powdered stubble or slapdash gowns, someone who sees through to the innocent soul like Grandma Eleanor always could.

Then again, she'd never seen him quite like this. When he'd worn her clothes, she'd viewed it as playtime, not knowing her grandson never wanted playtime to end. Lord, how he longs to walk the world in painful pumps, the breeze of freedom dancing through his long blonde hair and laying silky kisses on his cheeks. The best he does now is a ceiling fan and the wiry slaps of a wig he stole from a dumpster behind JC Penney's.

*Stole.* He, Father McKenzie, stole from the garbage to feed his sins.

His stomach lurches at the truth, and he pulls the blanket from the mirror. His face powder is splotchy. Patches are soft and white as a young bride, but the rough and ruddy skin between can't be mistaken for anything but a man's. The waltzing fantasy ends, and his partner disappears. But Kay Starr sings on, her *Wheel of Fortune* spinning, spinning, spinning. Leaning into the mirror, Edward sighs. Like Kay, he no longer dreams of winning.

With fifteen minutes before Saturday mass, Eleanor stands behind him, her hands on his shoulders. *Put on some lipstick, dear. Doll yourself up and greet the new day with joy. We'll walk together like we used to – proud and lovely.*

Edward shakes his head. As much as he wants it, he could never embody Eleanor like that. She looked most beautiful on Sunday strolls to St. Peter's, at the threshold between the world and worship. With sunlight on her back and God's light on her face, she was one of his angels. How could a man stuffed into women's clothing compare to an angel?

*No one cares what garments a soldier of Christ wears – just that he's true to his lord and congregation. I promise people will accept you, Edward. Don't you trust me?*

He nods, but his trust in her doesn't change the world around him, and the battle ends the way it always does. He pinches the false lashes from his eyes before splashing water on his face. Mascara runs through the ravines to his chin – trails of black tears that freckle the sink after falling. His wig removed and makeup gurgling down the drain, Edward dons his lovely lies again. It's hard to imagine anything more constricting than a corset, but the grief he wears with his vestments makes breathing difficult. He shuts his grandmother's Duska tin and snaps his collar closed, searching for the man of God in his reflection. With Eleanor's crucifix around his neck, God shines in silver, but Edward sees no man in the mirror.

Sunday, 12<sup>th</sup> January 2014

# You Can't Choose
# Your Friends

## by Shane Simmons

Sandra had some sort of 'breakdown' before the festive season. What with Stephen abandoning her just weeks before Christmas in favour of "that slut of a bastarding bitch," I've been lumbered with her for Christmas Day, Boxing Day, New Year's Eve, New Year's Day, oh, and most of the other days in between. We're almost halfway through the bloody month and I'm still tending to her histrionics.

"You're my 'life coach'. I need coaching back into life." From the glossy white floorboards she picks up the oversized wine glass I'd bought her for Christmas and downs its contents whole.

*Me?* She's selected *me* as her 'life coach'? Ha. Sandra makes me laugh, even with her panda eyes and random tears followed by outbursts of swearing. If age grants wisdom, then surely Sandra should have five years of foresight to explain why I'm not long twenty–two, and still I find myself with no one bar this scorned woman for adult company.

"I hate her. And I hate him. I HATE EVERYTHING!"

On a daily basis she screams, texts or finds some other way to relay her resentment to me. I'd suggest she hire one of those planes that writes fluffy messages in the sky to spell out the word

"CUNTS" over their love nest, but she'd kill me for resorting to any form of humour so early on in her heartbreak.

Heartbreak?

She pours a quarter glass of wine for me before snatching the bottle away to her vase–sized vessel. "Do you think they're happy? Do you? DO YOU?!"

I push out a sigh and crumple down into my shoulders, but as per, Sandra doesn't notice.

"They can't be happy because they're bastards! How could she do that to her own sister? Could you do that to your sister? COULD YOU?!"

Sandra's more than aware that my sister's husband is a putrid example of the male form. An oversized, balding figure who keeps the last precious strands of his hair in a halo that encircles his ball–shaped head. The idea of his greasy self makes me gag without too much effort. As Sandra stumbles out of the room, I rustle a bottle from the bag at my feet. I pour myself some rosé and swig it down. I had planned well: I'd bought one with a screw top. I only just slip it back in the bag before Sandra reappears with yet another box of tissues.

"Aren't you drinking?" She eyes up my empty glass and glances down at the two barren bottles by her feet. Of which I'd only tasted a few drops. "How could he? Just, how could he? Do you know how long they were shagging for, behind my back? DO YOU?!" She punctuates each word with a finger, jabbing in my direction, her face plumped and purplish, as if Satan himself will burst forth from under her skin.

"NO! NO I DON'T! And *you* need to stop screaming at *me* about all this!"

She stops jabbing the air and stares. Her finger curls up into her fist.

"Oh, it's like that is it?" she whispers, slurring. "I need some company after my man has left me, for my BLOODY SISTER, and you can't be arsed?" She topples around, grabbing hold of the mantel but maintaining her glare.

"Seeing as you told me how you shagged his cousin in the toilets at some wedding reception months before the two of you split up, I think you're being a bit of a hypocrite!"

"Get out." Swivelling on the spot, she points in the vague direction of the door. "Just go!"

I pick up my bag and coat from the sofa.

"Fuck off. Fuck off!! Fuck off!!! FUCK OFF!!!!" she yells, and drops to the floor.

"You mad drunken cow." I step over her and walk out. As the door slams behind me I hear her shrieks wither into sobs and I pause on the landing. Should I go back in and get her up and off to bed? Tomorrow she won't even remember what's happened.

I descend the stairs and her whimpers disappear behind me. I step through the hall she shares with her neighbours and head out the front door into the crispest January night. I'm only two minutes around the corner from home, but I take the long way just to draw in lungful after deep lungful of biting London air.

# Cornfield

## by Michelle Elvy

When a story begins with a blowjob in the back seat of a stolen car, you can bet on how it will end. There will be a high−speed chase scene, profanity, cops, *those fuckers*, trying to fuck things up, and a broken heart, or at least one sore dick. But this is not that kind of story. This is a story not about the stolen car or the guy driving it or the boyfriend of the girl in the backseat, or the boy who gets the blowjob (who's not the boyfriend). This story's more about the boy sitting in the backseat who simply unlocked the car so his friends could speed away on a joyride. This is the story about the boy who's not even sure why he's there with them. This is the story about the boy who goes along for the ride and sits in the back seat while one friend drives like a maniac and the other sits with feet on the dash and lights up a joint and the third eventually ends up with that blow job, when the boyfriend of the girl, the one in the front seat, is too stoned to care. This is the story of the boy who sits in the car racing down the highway, who dreams of something so far away and so incongruous and far−fetched he's never mentioned it. This is the story of the boy who sits in the backseat of a stolen car speeding down a Maryland highway on a cold January morning who dreams of Cape Horn.

"Shit. It doesn't fit."

"Try from another angle."

"C'mon, Stevie, you gotta apply more pressure."

Stevie is trying to tune out the trio behind him. They have plenty of advice as always, but it's only Stevie who knows how to break into a car in record time. It's not that hard, but none of his pals has the patience or skill to maneuver the Slim Jim just so, especially in the stone grey pre–dawn of a winter morning. He knows which cars to choose – better if they're from the 90s, even earlier if possible. The newer models are no good, too much electronic fancywork, GPS tracking and all that shit. He likes old–fashioned cars, the kind his dad used to drive, big and metallic and not all plasticy. He learned with a coathanger on cars with big windows and locking mechanisms with obvious knobs, but he can crack into the smaller Japanese models too. Anyone could, really. Except his friends.

He's used to their background noise, but on this day they are just standing around, hands in pockets and lips flapping while he freezes his fingers off.

"Shut the fuck up, guys!"

"Yeah, let the master work!" chides Lucky, who's been called that ever since he got nabbed by the cops for selling drugs a few years back when it's his older brother who is the real criminal of the family. Lucky's no criminal. Lucky just likes weed a little too much.

Stevie shoots Lucky a look: "Dick."

Lucky comes back with the best – and, if you're Lucky, *only* – comeback for *Dick*: "Pussy."

Stevie ends the conversation: *Click.*

"Who's calling my boy a pussy now?" says Manny as he pushes past Stevie and hops in the driver's seat. At eighteen,

Manny is all bravado and bulging biceps, and imagines himself the leader of this unlikely group of bandits. Manny always drives.

The others climb into the car and are soon heading down Route 2, out of town and rolling on long straight roads through the old tobacco country of South County. "Where to, boys?" asks Manny. "All the way!" comes the answer, always the same.

Sometimes *all the way* is as far as the Safeway parking lot, because Rick has to get to work by 7am and can't afford to lose this job, even though he plays bad–ass but really is the biggest pussy of all. Rick is a twin and can't seem to shake the idea that he's the smaller and weaker of the two brothers. Rick is what Mannie calls 'soft'. Rick is afraid much of the time. But Rick is probably the meanest of the lot.

Sometimes *all the way* is as far as the Galesville Market, where they stop for ham and cheese subs and Old Harry, the owner, gives them each a gumball because their enthusiasm is something he doesn't see much of these days and he always thinks them younger than they really are – never mind the fact that they show up in a different car each time. Old Harry likes the way they giggle: boys being irrepressible boys and slapping each other on the back. He does not see them as delinquents. He does not even consider that it's a Monday morning and they should be in school. He just sees boys who are hungry on a bitter January morning.

Today they stop by Ellie's and she nestles into the back seat between Rick and Stevie. She leans to the right onto Rick's shoulder and yawns, but Stevie is sure he feels her thigh press against his. Manny keeps driving, faster than usual, as corn and sorghum speed by. Lucky rolls a joint but only he and Rick take part, passing it back and forth, front to back and front again. Lucky turns around and grins at his girl and at Stevie but can't see Rick so passes the joint up over his head again. A half–hour goes by and Lucky falls asleep and Manny drives faster and Stevie squishes himself into his own corner of the backseat when he sees Ellie reach her hand down Rick's pants.

"Seriously, Manny, where're we goin'?" says Rick from the back seat, just making conversation all cool while Lucky's girl gets busy in his pants, but just then there's more to worry about than an errant handjob as blue and red lights come flashing behind.

"Shit."

"Hang on," says Manny, and veers off down a side road. A sharp turn comes up too quickly and the car swerves. Ellie squeals and is thrown right but when the car straightens out and Manny resumes driving fast along another short straightaway, she doesn't come up for air.

Stevie is now struggling to keep his eyes forward. He's used to all the fuck−ups but this is not his kind of game. He thinks he might be sick. He's not sure whether it's Manny swerving again or the idea of Rick getting blown at 9am in the seat beside him. He rolls his window down and leans his head out into the freezing wind. His ears feel like they'll fall off but he dares not come back in. Lucky's passed out up front, and next to him they aren't even trying to be quiet anymore; Rick's making little sobbing noises and Ellie's head's bobbing more exuberantly.

Even worse, Stevie's about to look despite his best intentions.

But he's saved from his own depravity when the car lurches hard to the right and the next thing he knows he's airborne, tossed like a ragdoll and soaring across acres of a desolate winter cornfield.

The dreams are always like this. He's lifted on a blanket of warmth, surrounded by a frozen January sky. Great Grandpa Gus, the one who worked on whaling ships, floats by but is too far away to hear Stevie's call. Stevie is cushioned on clouds like cotton candy and Gus is rioting along in heavy seas below. Stevie reaches out a hand to grab the ship's rigging but as he extends his arm the canvas tears with a screeching sound and he watches helplessly as first the topsail flutters away in the wind and then the ship turns inside out, halyards howling and rigging wrenching angrily from the decks and flying up with the sails. The great heavy hull is the last to go – lifted from the dark ocean and rising up, up, up, set twirling in the tornado–black air. Stevie tries to call for Great Grandpa Gus but panic rises in his gut because his voice won't reach from southern Anne Arundel County, on January 13, 2014, to Cape Horn where a great sailing ship is tearing apart at the seams nearly a century before.

The world slows and both ship and clouds disappear and all that is left is the cornfield now rising at an alarming speed upward toward him. In one instant Stevie thinks he sees fire off to the side and he may even hear music – *Nothing lasts forever but the earth and sky* – underneath the screeching tires and burning rubber and crunching metal. But he's not sure because he closes his eyes, only for a moment, and things go black.

When Stevie wakes in the hospital near midnight and his father says, "Where've you been, son?" and his mother covers him in kisses saying, "My darling child!" his mind first flashes to Manny and Lucky and Rick and Ellie and then he reaches once more for Gus. He tries to recall the cornfield over Maryland – or was it Kansas? – and he wants to say something about dust or wind but instead he replies, "Cape Horn".

Tuesday, 14<sup>th</sup> January 2014

# Storm Lake

## by Len Kuntz

The storm hit without warning, and now snowdrifts as tall as four feet are blocking the front door.

I try to call my wife but there's no cell service. Today's our anniversary: seven years. She's in Baltimore for a convention. When she returns we're supposed to make a decision about whether we're too broken to mend, her having had an affair with her boss, me being too scared to leave her.

Snow continues to drop, thick as mud, plates of the stuff. Outside tree branches break every half hour or so, the wreckage sounding like thunder and gunfire.

The power's been out since evening. Rotten food odors fill the kitchen. The refrigerator leaks dirty water. The silence in the house is so still it's unnerving, and now I can see my breath.

The dog stares at me, her head cocked, as if she senses doom. When I let her piss in the house, then mop up the floor, she scampers to a corner and begins mewling.

Outside, the lake is a white shelf, an ivory island. Ducks – looking more like decoys than the real things – cluster in the northeastern corner. Part of me wishes I owned a gun.

Our house in the woods is set a mile back from any road, and I know no one will be coming soon. Power outages in these parts can take days to be repaired.

The dog starts to moan, as if it's sick or injured or possessed. When I toss a sock at her, she shreds the thing in an instant.

The marriage counselor my wife and I tried always seemed to take my wife's side. He said my wife's motivations for the affair could be numerous. He suggested I was, in many ways, more than responsible. He said men who ignore their spouses are asking for trouble.

When I look over at the dog, she's chewing the leg of a stuffed chair and staring at me, growling as she rips off splinters. "Have at it," I say.

I ball up old newspapers and my wife's *Vogue* magazines and start a fire in the sink. I go to the bedroom and rummage through her dresser drawers, returning with lacy bras and thongs, most with the price tags still on. They're slow to catch flame, smoldering a ghostlike smoke.

When I was a kid, my brother and I used to walk across the lake when it froze over. He'd go out the farthest, mocking my cowardice. I told him I'd heard another boy had fallen through the ice, but that only caused my brother to titter and call me chicken shit.

The homes across the shore all have their lights on. It's a half mile trek. I get my coat and hat and boots. I walk through mattresses of snow, down a slope to the frozen waterfront. I look back at the house, hooded with drifts of gleaming white. I tell it goodbye and I think I mean it.

Wednesday, 15<sup>th</sup> January 2014

# First Inning

## by Michael Webb

I awaken in the middle of a dream, pursued by wolves in a lonely, arctic forest, emerging from the phantasmagoria of dream life into my bedroom full of polished wood, the black empty flatscreen TV, and a forlorn action figure on its side on the floor. Usually I don't sleep heavy enough to miss out on a kid invasion, but apparently I did today. I sit up, shaking my head to clear it.

Stretching out my throwing arm without thinking about it, pinwheeling it around in a big arc, I work the sleep out of the muscles. I play with it constantly. All pitchers do. You listen for pops or cracks, sore spots, adhesions, anything that might impede throwing a ball at high speed. We have to do everything perfectly, repeating the same series of motions thousands of times in a year. Making your living with your body, you are on a knife−edge, ready for the imperfection that would head you towards your final pitch.

I pull a red Diamondbacks shirt on from a couple of springs ago, thinking about how much looser it used to fit, and stumble downstairs. I hear the familiar buzz of voices, inane chatter from my daughter, more coherent speech from my son, my wife's voice with the edge of authority in it, keeping them on task. It sounds foreign to my ears, even after all these years – spending 7 or 8 months a year mostly away from them makes me a stranger in my own life.

Around the corner and into the kitchen, all gleaming metal and burnished wood, I see them all, buzzing through the morning with practiced precision. Angela has a very short tennis skirt on, her legs still hard and toned like the cheerleader she was.

"I'm playing tennis with Marissa today. I figured we wouldn't wake you," she says. Marissa Adler is married to Steven Adler, a fellow Arizona State alum, a part time outfielder who took me deep in extra innings in Baltimore the last time I faced him. We are still friends, although he seldom lets me forget about how he beat me.

"Thanks, dear," I say.

Coffee is still warm in the pot, and I pour myself a cup. The kids eye me up and down. The younger one, Maddie, is almost scowling. It's still unclear to her what I do, and she still finds my presence strange. She is never entirely ready to trust me. Not yet.

"You have APC today?" Angela asks. Athletic Performance Center: the scientists, nutritionists, physical therapists, and sadistic personal trainers whose job it is to prepare my body, and specifically my shoulder, elbow, and wrist, for the months of work they have in front of them.

"Yeah," I say. "11 to 1."

"So you can pick them up? I need to go to Macy's to look for a dress for that event on Saturday." In the favor–trading world of professional sports, I had agreed to attend a charity dinner for the Phoenix Suns' foundation in exchange for some NBA tickets. I don't want to go, but fair is fair, plus Angela loves getting dressed up.

"Sure, hon. No problem."

"Did you hear that, Madison? Daddy will pick you up today, not Mommy."

My daughter looks uncertain, her tiny face forming around a frown. "But Mommy! Miss Rose say ..." Madison hates surprises. You have to lay out a schedule for her every day, so she knows what to expect. Our son Dylan, on the other hand, couldn't care less, taking bumps in the road with a surfer's easy calm.

Angela cuts her off. "Miss Rose knows your father, Maddie. It's fine. Trust me. He's allowed to do pickups."

"OK," she says, unconvinced.

I see a stray lace on Madison's tiny pink sneaker. I bend low to tie it.

Angela continues bustling, preparing lunches and school bags, wiping noses and taming cowlicks. I watch the house function as it must while I am away. Dylan is concentrating on his cereal, taking enormous bites and chewing them slowly, a small smile on his lips. I have never seen anyone enjoy food as much as he does.

"Would you get Dylan's inhaler, hun? It's in the −" Angela begins.

"I got it, Mom," Dylan says between slurps of milk, pointing to a silver case next to his school bag.

"Oh," she says, surprised. "Good boy, Dyl. Thanks."

Then Madison jerks her foot away with a snarl. "Noooooo," she insists. "Mommy do it!" I feel a tiny pang of fear and hurt at her sharp tone. I understood intellectually that it is hard for her, that Ange does things one way, and they're used to that. But the rejection stings. Angela stops on her way through, stooping so she shows me a flash of her upper thigh, her polished short fingernails darting as she ties the wayward lace without a word.

They are ready a few minutes later, lining up as I put the milk back into the refrigerator and wash the kids' dishes. Ange always tells me I don't have to do that, because she spends all of my money, but I feel like I have to do something.

"Say goodbye to Daddy," Angela says as she herds them out the door.

"Bye, Dad!" Dylan says brightly.

"Bye," Madison says, and they leave. I listen to their footsteps crunch down the drive, their voices loud and bright again. I wonder about how I have become the interloper, even while I do bring home the large checks that pay for the house and the cars and the food and the private schools and the trips to Disney. The house echoes with silence, and I shrug and go upstairs to change into exercise wear.

Another year of large numbers beckons.

# Making Music

## by James Claffey

The Bird wakes with the sound of the dawn chorus, birds chattering on the telephone wires outside his window. On the floor, the Holy Water bottle; the events of the previous night return to his memory in full, terrible Technicolor. He makes a promise to go straight up to the Parish Priest's house that very morning and see what Father O'Hehir will make of his troubled night.

The town is clad in a cloak of dust and boredom as he moseys up Main Street towards the small stone church on the corner of Market Street. A brindled bitch lies in the shadow of the Bank of Ireland, nursing three scrawny pups, and the Bird thinks for a moment that the one who fights the other two off the teat mightn't make a decent fighting dog. The dog's persistence is exactly the quality needed in a good fighter. But training them to inflict harm on other dogs is an awful amount of work he thinks, and gives his head a shake.

His beard itches, and when he runs a dry tongue across his lips, the salty—sweet taste of day—old beans reminds him of how little money he has in the biscuit jar on the kitchen dresser. Never mind, he thinks, as he moseys through the church gates and into the dark entryway where the white marble font he's dipped his fingers into all his life sits. He pushes the double doors open and enters the echoing church as Father O'Hehir limps across the altar, genuflecting half—way, and continuing towards the sacristy entrance. Four silent confession boxes flank the back of the church, the dark chocolate wood stained with the absorbed sins of so many years. The Bird coughs. The echo stops the priest in mid—step.

"How's the Bird?" Father O'Hehir asks, walking through the gilded altar gates and up the aisle towards his visitor.

"Grand, thanks be to God," the Bird replies. "Though, I wanted to have a word with you about the Mammy." The Bird stumbles on the words. He fingers the collar of his shirt. "Well, it's a … it's … it's a bit delicate, Father," he says. "But, since the funerals I've been having nightmares, and I'm certain the Mammy is visiting the house at night."

"By the Hokey, that's a powerful tale altogether," the priest says, his eyebrows aquiver. "Are you sure it's not the rats in the attic you're after hearing?"

"Now, Father, I'm after seeing my own Mammy these past nights. Didn't she only appear to me as if she was an angel from Heaven?"

"Was it a dream you were having?" the priest asks.

"Father, as God's my witness, she fluttered her wings and shook her tail feathers at me from the bedstead."

The priest scratches his chin, raises and lowers his eyebrows twice and beckons to the Bird to follow. From a recess in the holy water font he takes a plastic bottle in the shape of the Blessed Virgin Mary and fills it with water. "There now, sprinkle this across the windows and the threshold of the door to the bedroom and you'll be game ball."

"What if that doesn't work, Father?" the Bird asks, sliding the bottle into his pocket.

"We'll cross that bridge when we come to it, won't we," the priest says, with a knowing wink.

The Bird runs a hand through his sandy hair and heads off toward his house, the distant rainclouds unloading their burden on the green hills to the south. He passes along by the large façade of McKettrick's Public House and thinks he might have a jar, but frets that if he doesn't take care of the holy water, he'll have another restless night.

Inside the house once more, he creeps upstairs, the opened bottle held in front of him like a burning stake. The bedroom is dim and on the bed his mother's nightgown lies crushed in a ball. Kneeling, the Bird recites a decade of the Holy Rosary and takes the bottle of Holy Water and scatters it in the closet. Small trails of vapor rise from the wooden boards. "Oh, Mammy, are you trapped in there?" he asks. Not a sound, only the rapid beating of his own heart. "Hail Holy Queen, Mother of Mercy, Hail our life, our sweetness, and our hope," he intones, spraying the water on the windowsill and then across the foot of the door. His duty done, he shakes out the nightdress and folds it neatly, placing it under the pillow.

Maybe later, he thinks, he will take a bicycle ride over to Clara for the *seisiún* in Hogan's Bar. Thursdays, local fiddlers, bodhrán players, and tin whistlers get together in the main bar around the fire and play until closing time. More often than not there are some of the town's young girls gathered in bunches, like spring flowers at the Saturday market in Mullingar. He holds out hopes of meeting a husky young one with wide hips and a straight smile, who might overlook his under-bite and pay him a little attention.

As a boy, he'd had no luck with the girls. Partly because his father was the town undertaker, and most of the town's children were afraid of "catching death" if they touched the Bird, or even came close. When he told his mother that he hated what his father did for a living she only hugged him tight and said he'd had no choice in the matter since his father's family had been burying the local population for over 150 years.

At the local dances, hops, and other social occasions he finds himself alone at the side of the room, wallflowering it, and sucking his drink through a straw. The Bird prefers the outskirts of the crowd, staying to himself, nursing his pint and sneaking looks at the pretty girls from under his cap; even though he's had Murtagh the Solicitor sell the business after the parents' funerals, he knows the locals will always associate him with the burying of the dead.

Hogan's is hopping when the Bird arrives. Punters at the bar are three deep and he elbows his way into the throng and waves a fiver about for an age before Breda, the owner's wife, gives him a smile and tilts a pint glass under the tap.

"Busy night, Breda," he says. "Is the *seisiún* about to start?"

"It is, Bird, it is. We're waiting for the lass on the tin whistle to arrive. French she is."

"By God, is that a fact? French, and playing the *feadóg*?" the Bird replies. He's learned a tune or two on the old brass pipe, but hasn't much aptitude for music. Still, he enjoyed the traditional music, grew up with it on the radio, and wasn't his daddy a great one for the *seisiúns*.

"Aye. She's a Breton, I hear they're descendants of the Celts, down there," Breda says, and rushes to the other end of the bar where another customer waves a note in the air.

With his pint in his hand, the Bird makes his way to the wall adjacent to the toilets, where he can enjoy the music and slip out the emergency exit should he want to get off home early. The distance home is a good five miles, and on the bicycle in the dark will be a treacherous one. As he settles into his corner, the musicians tune their instruments, and he admires the way the fiddle player pings the strings with his little fingernail. A sparrow–like woman with grey hair winds her way through the crowd and sits on a short stool with the other musicians. She undoes the clasps of a small, narrow box and pulls out a shiny tin whistle.

"Good of you to put in an appearance, Melody, even if you are a bit on the late side," one of the players ribs her.

"My name is not Melody," she says, under her breath.

"Ah, lighten up on her, doesn't she come farther than all of us? Go on, Noreen, get her a glass of Guinness and blackcurrant would you?" the bodhrán player orders his wife.

A bucketful of reels and airs later the Bird goes to the toilet and relieves himself standing at the porcelain urinal where he reads the sports pages of the newspaper behind a Perspex cover. When he returns to the bar the woman with the long gray hair is just outside the exit on a steel Guinness barrel smoking a cigarette. The Bird sucks in his gut and sticks out his chest, intent on making a good impression, and after coughing so as not to startle her, he says, "You've quite a pair of lips on you, if you don't mind me saying so."

"Thank you. Though I don't know if you're talking about my playing, or whether you want to kiss me down below!" the woman replies, in a slight foreign accent.

"Oh, no! I m ... mea ... meant your music. I apologize," the Bird says, stuttering.

"Now I should be disappointed, no?" she says. "My name is Elodie." She holds a hand out for him to shake.

"Pleased to meet you, I'm sure. I'm called the Bird. The Bird Mahony," he says, and takes her small hand in his and shakes it once. He blushes, not quite knowing what to say next.

"What a curious name, Bird? Why are you called Bird?"

"Oh, my mammy said when I was born I looked just like a baby chicken, so they called me Bird, and never anything else."

"I think it's a lovely name, Bird." She smiles again. "You have traveled far to hear the music, Bird?"

"The next town over. Sure, it's only five miles." The Bird runs a finger inside his collar and feels the sweat around his neck. "Well, I must be going now, it's a long cycle back home." He puts a thumb and forefinger to the peak of his cap and nods at her.

"Well, I do hope you come to hear us again," she says, smiling at him. She stubs the cigarette butt with the toe of her boot and wanders back to the other musicians. The Bird looks into the space she's occupied, for a full minute, until the strains of Cooley's reel wafts out on the night air. Whistling softly, he slips out to his bicycle, clips the trousers about his ankles and mounts with a grunt. As he pedals the narrow road home a light rain falls and he whistles all the louder.

# The Suicide Club

## by Gwendolyn Joyce Mintz

You'd think Mora's smoking something other than a cigarette by the way she jumps when she hears me behind her.

"Damn, Aaron," she says, shaking her head from side to side. "You scared me."

"Sorry." I push the gate to the fencing that surrounds the dumpster open and heave the garbage–filled bag into the metal container.

Mora has one arm tight around her waist for warmth, the hand of the other, balancing a cigarette before her face.

"Why're you over here?"

"Scott said we can't smoke by the back door anymore; it doesn't look good for customers." She rolls her eyes and takes another drag.

"I thought you gave up smoking this year."

"My New Year's resolutions last about a day, two if I'm lucky."

I chuckle, close the gate and replace the chain.

"What about you?" Mora asks. "You make any resolutions you can't keep?"

"Nope. I made one and so far, I'm good."

"That's why you've advanced here and I'm still just above minimum wage." She takes a last puff, drops the butt on the ground and squashes it with the toe of her shoe. "So what is it?

I'm curious."

I hesitate. Then taking care with my words, I say, "I, uhm, I'm not planning on being here another year. I've resolved to get things in order so I can go."

"Lucky you. I wish I could leave this place. Where're you headed – another job in town or you're leaving altogether?"

I glance up at the sky.

"I won't tell Scott. Hell, he deserves to lose a good worker like you."

I take a breath. I can trust Mora. I know I can.

"I'm going ... Mora, I'm going ..."

She raises a brow.

"I'm going to kill myself. I'm getting things in order so I won't be here, alive, after this year."

She examines my face. A whispered "wow" escapes her lips.

I think, in the minutes that pass, that I should go back in but my feet have frozen in place.

Mora fumbles with the cigarette carton in her pocket. She takes another and lights it. After a few drags, she says, "Sometimes I wish ..." She glances at me. "When I got out after the second time, I really believed that things would get better, that I could make them better." She shakes her head and looks away.

"I know. I don't know how to change things either, to get them to change. I've tried but I'm done."

She faces me. "Would you have said goodbye?"

"I was planning to, yes."

"Do you know when?"

"Nah. Just when some things are in order."

"You are so much braver than me." Mora flicks the half-smoked cigarette to the ground. She stomps it out and walks away.

§

My shift's done before Mora's and she stops me at the time clock. Asks what I'm doing now that I'm off.

Going home.

"Let's go get a drink at Kelly's."

I stare at her and maybe she can read me because she says, "Yes, I want to talk about it but I'm not going to try and talk you out of it. I'm off in half an hour. Meet me, okay?"

She's up to something but I agree to meet.

"One?" the hostess asks, her hand hovering over the stacked menus on the podium.

"I'm meeting someone. But we won't be eating, probably just drinks." I eat free at work – I'm not paying for another meal. This is one thing noted on my list of 'THINGS I WILL MISS'. Although I know I won't even be aware, but that's beside the point.

"Sit at the bar or do you want a table?"

I take the table. I need the space between me and Mora so I won't feel so vulnerable.

"Your server will be right with you."

"Thanks," I say as I'm stripping my jacket off. Before I place it on the back of the chair, I watch the hostess walk away and note that great asses will be another thing missed.

I'm still sipping at my draft beer when Mora bustles in. She glances around, finally zooms in on my raised arm flagging her. It's not until she's at the table that I realize she's not alone.

Alarm must flood my face because suddenly Mora is

apologizing and reassuring.

"This is Diane," she says. "I met her at the psychiatric hospital."

I don't know if she was a patient or a worker. "You tried to kill yourself too?"

Diane nods.

I turn to Mora.

She avoids my eyes, peels off her coat. She and Diane pull out chairs. They sit on either side of me.

I raise the mug to my lips. I give Mora time to explain. But before she does, the server pops up. Mora orders a Bloody Mary and Diane, a soft drink.

When the three of us are alone again, Mora says, "Diane needs someone to talk to."

I turn to Diane. She's fiddling with her hands.

I'm pissed at Mora, though I'm not sure why. I grunt then spit out, "She needs to talk but you're talking for her?"

Mora jerks back a bit. She turns to Diane. Back to me. "Damn, Aaron."

"No, damn you, Mora," I tell her. "I'm not a freaking counse –"

"I want to die," Diane interjects. "Or not live the way I'm living. Either way, I, I just want someone I can share that with. Someone who's not going to try and talk me out of it."

"I just thought maybe the three of us could talk about it sometimes," Mora says. "I haven't decided completely that that isn't the road for me, but it'd be easier to talk to someone who understands because they want the same thing."

The server returns with the drinks.

We drink in silence.

Putting down my mug, I mutter, "A suicide club."

Mora chuckles. "Yeah, I guess."

I turn the empty mug in circles. Watch the water drops it leaves behind.

The irritation I felt is replaced with some kind of calm. I feel close to these two simply because we're tired of fighting alone.

"Fine," I say.

"Then we'll meet again? Let's say in a month? See where we're at?" Mora suggests.

I bite the inside of my lip for a moment, then bob my head up and down.

"Although," Diane adds, "it would make me happy if I couldn't make it."

Saturday, 18th January 2014

# Compassion

## by Stephen V. Ramey

Anne closed the curtains at precisely 10:30 this morning. She's only trying to slow the heat leaking from these old wooden window frames, but sometimes I think she thinks she can control entropy. The downside is that it leaves me in a dim room with twelve–foot–high ceilings. I haven't even bothered to push the lever that opens the recliner.

My father died November 11, 2002, but he was diagnosed on January 18, 2000. To me, that day – today, January 18 – is the meaningful one, the day his death took root.

Footsteps sound upstairs. Anne must be done reading her email. I imagine boards denting and rebounding as her steps continue onto the staircase. Panic shoots through me. My eyes seek the tablet in sleep mode on my lap. How long have I been sitting here? Fifteen minutes? An hour? Anne will want to see progress.

I touch the touchpad, and work through the memorized motions of making the computer aware of me. The word processor page takes form. I feel a moment of hope. Maybe I started writing before ... but, no, it's blank.

A stair tread cries out. Anne's hand appears on the railing. *Type something!*

*I ...* But it's so trite, to open with "I". I press Backspace, and the page is blank again.

Anne stops at the threshold between rooms. We recently removed carpet from the dining room, and were pleased to find the original wood flooring in good shape. I wish I could say the same for the living room. We took up this carpet last year. The pine boards were dinged and scraped, warped in a few places. We covered the worst with an inexpensive area rug.

"Well?" she says.

"It's starting to come together," I say. I'm supposed to write a letter to the editor about the city's plans to demolish another building. In the five years we've lived here, three buildings have come down in the downtown district, leaving gaps in the Victorian era façade like extracted teeth. If this continues we'll have no smile, nothing left to connect us to our glorious past. Once, New Castle rivaled Pittsburgh in industry, and boasted the largest tin mill in the world.

"Read what you have so far," Anne says. Her voice is flat. She knows.

"I ..." I stare at the floor.

Anne takes down our coats from the rack beside the door, and tosses mine across the room. It lands in a heap. "We're going for a walk."

"Okay." I set the tablet aside. My stomach mimics a clenching fist. I love my wife, but it's so easy to despise her too.


"Why are you having problems this time?" Anne says. She digs gloves from her coat pocket and pulls them on.

A shiver comes over me. It's cold enough out here to make me realize how warm it was inside. I ball my hands into my pockets as we pass the Pizza Hut and start across Grant Street toward the more historic sections of downtown. The sky is a continuous layer of cloud, but bright despite it. Probably because I've been indoors all morning.

"I can't find an interesting way into the piece," I say. I've never been close to my muse. Lately it's been a struggle just to glimpse her wing dust.

"It's just a letter to the editor," Anne says. Her gaze is dull as pewter. I remember when her eyes used to shine, or was that my imagination? A bus growls past, water splashing from its tires. An advertisement shows a happy family. *Refresh Dental brings out your best smile.*

"You're supposed to be a writer," Anne says. "Half the letters they publish wouldn't pass a third grade grammar test."

"It has to be good," I say. I watch my black sneaker step up onto the crumbling sidewalk. We have slate by our house. It's cracked too, but that took a hundred years of wear. This concrete was poured since we moved here. "What's the point of writing something just to write it?"

"The point is that you agreed to do this for the Historic District Board," Anne says. "That's the point."

I blow a warm, moist breath into my hands. *Did she forget my gloves on purpose?* "All the more reason it should be good," I say.

"What it should be," Anne says, "is *finished*. The meeting is tonight. You were supposed to send it in last week."

"I know, I know." I hang my head. I'm wearing sneakers with Velcro instead of laces. How lazy is that? My toes are cold. I look up.

A half-block ahead, the traffic signal turns red, and the red cascades block after block after block. This part of New Castle isn't much different from most small cities: a funeral home, a 1960's office complex, traffic lights. Even here, though, there are signs. The church across the way, with its turrets and crenellated roofline, brings to mind Conquistadors. The next block features a towering Catholic church with stained glass windows that recall Renaissance artwork. Victorian houses–turned businesses dot the neighborhood, the stiff formality of their construction offset by complex steeple rooflines and gingerbread trim painted in primary colors.

"You'll finish when we get back," Anne says. "I thought it might be helpful to walk past the building."

"I'm not sure anything will help," I mumble.

We pass the Humburg Insurance building, a low slung seventies design with angled plate glass and wood shingle siding. Snow speckled with black cinders is piled within the shadow of its eaves. I wonder if New Castle isn't like that, stained with the past and slow to melt. Maybe that's why I'm having problems.

"Hey!" A woman waves from across the street.

"Rose," Anne says.

A smile overtakes me. I wave back. Rose is Italian and finds more reasons to laugh than to frown. I like her. She's also a witch.

"I wish you would smile like that for me," Anne says.

"I wish I could," I say. She winces and I want to take it back. I don't mean to be passive-aggressive, it just slips out sometimes.

We watch Rose bustle across four lanes, bundled in winter boots, coat, gloves, and a floppy knitted hat that hides her gender. Nothing, however, can mask her energy.

"How are you guys doing?" she says. She stomps slush from her boots, then dips past my guard to give me a hug. There's an intoxicating aspect to Rose's spontaneous hugs. No manipulation, no ulterior motive, just the bliss that comes from being momentarily aware of a compassionate universe. I squeeze back, but that adds nothing.

Rose steps back. "Jimmy and I danced beneath the full moon on Thursday."

"Naked?" I say.

She laughs. "Do I look stupid?" She rubs her gloved hands together, then slaps them. "Are you guys coming to Jimmy's gig tonight?"

"Where?" Anne says.

"Cracker Barrel, seven−ish."

"I didn't know Cracker Barrel did live comedy," I say. *Especially Jimmy's irreverent satire.*

Rose gives us a Mona Lisa smile. "They don't know it either. It's part of his Stealth Comedy Tour where he goes into a business and does a routine. We're going to record it for his webcast. I'm in charge of that."

"Sounds interesting," I say. "Count me in." The Cracker Barrel is about fifteen minutes east, near WalMart, Lowes, Staples and other capitalist vampires.

"You're not going anywhere until you finish your work," Anne says. She nods to Rose. "He's grounded."

My whole body tenses. "I'm not a child, Anne."

"Prove it," she says.

"Ouch," Rose chimes in. "There's a spell for writer's block, you know." She bites the end of a gloved finger, pulls off the glove with her teeth, and produces a Smartphone from her pocket.

"You have it on your phone?" I say.

"You've never heard of Google? Some writer you are." She swipes and types, then extends the phone toward me. There's a list of ingredients, and more than a page of instruction.

"Looks complicated."

"If this stuff was easy, anyone would do it."

I push the phone away. "It's not actually writer's block. Fourteen years ago today, Dad got his cancer diagnosis."

Anne frowns. "Why didn't you tell me?"

"I shouldn't have to. I told you last year, and the year before that, probably."

"I'm sorry," Rose says. She puts the phone away. "Is he, did he ... pass?"

"Two days before his seventieth birthday," Anne says. She doesn't like to be caught without the facts of a situation.

"That's so sad," Rose says.

"It's been twelve years," Anne says. "And they weren't even close. Mostly, I think it's an excuse not to write."

"She wants me to demolish my father's memory," I say, "but insists I write letters when the city plans to tear down one lousy building. Doesn't that seem hypocritical to you?"

"A building dies with its destruction, and deserves our protection," Rose says. "Your father isn't gone, Stephen. You shouldn't let grief block out the light." She glances to the sky. "If you want, I can help you let go."

"Seriously?" Anne says. "That's what he needs."

"Gee, thanks," I say. "It's nice to have supportive friends and family."

Rose grabs my hand. "You have to ask yourself," she says, "whether a person does a blind man any favors by polishing his cane."

"I don't know what that means."

She shrugs. "We can either pay lip service to what you believe is important, or we can try to open our eyes to what *is* important. People who cling to ghosts are avoiding something in their reality."

"He's afraid of something," Anne says. "Failure, maybe?"

"Oh, it's more than that," Rose says. She presses my hand to her cheek. I feel my fingers unclench, cup her warm flesh.

Anne's expression dissolves into a stunned stare. Her eyes cast at me, cling, repel. Her lips push together. *She's jealous*, I think. *Afraid.*

# The Storm

## by Gay Degani

If a stranger stands, say, on the top of the creek bank in wooly darkness, he might wonder about the cabins, so oddly placed on this residential street. Vacation rentals built a hundred years back, five of them, plainly shingled, form a U around a weedy courtyard. On the other side of a thick border of Eugenia trees, a Mediterranean mansion sits on a knoll. Other homes along the road belong to a middle world, neither imposing nor humble, built in the thirties when the nearness of Riolito Creek seemed a special place to live until a dam and flood channel changed the natural swell and ebb of the creek and stole much of its natural beauty. On the edge of the city, far from schools, homes mismatched and unkempt, the neighborhood has become less and less desirable.

This stranger, unmindful of the growing wind, might notice Jamie in the front cabin, holding aside the curtain, hair clipped back from her neck, the yellow light from behind turning her to silhouette. It's too dark for the stranger to see the crease between her brows, the grim set of her mouth, but what tells him everything, is the sliding slope of her shoulders.

Leaves skitter along the Old Road. A gust rustles through sycamore and oak. Jamie turns away. The abandoned curtain sways.

Lily and Collin watch "Sesame Street" on the VCR Sean brought back from one of his trips, "Property of Lincoln Motel" scratched into the back. What will he bring this time? Ice bucket? Shower curtain? Those little soaps and shampoos and plastic–wrapped cups that make the kids squeal when he empties his pockets?

"I'm hungry," says Lily from her spot on the carpet.

Jamie says, "Okay, sweetie," but before heading into the kitchen, she checks the window again. Only blackness. A whoosh of wind rattles the windows; a door slams across the courtyard at Mr. German's, a light pops on.

"Mom." Impatience from Lily. "Hungry."

Jamie puts the kids to bed and checks her cell. Nothing from Sean.

He said he'd be home tonight, but maybe not tonight, "maybe" meaning go to bed and don't think about it. Not this time. She's sick of being let down. She tiptoes into the kids' room, slides open drawers, and quietly pulls out underwear, t–shirts, jeans, sweatshirts.

A groggy "Mom?" comes from Lily's bed.

Jamie says, "Go to sleep."

Flicking off the living room light with her elbow, Jamie remembers shoes for the kids. Decides to get them tomorrow and heads into her own room, dumps the clothes on the bed, and drags her big blue Samsonite from the closet. She has no relatives except for an aunt in Oregon, but she hesitates to go there. If she leaves Sean, she doesn't want to be found. At least not until she clears her head. She told Lily if Daddy didn't come by tomorrow, they'd get in the car and join him for a mini–vacation. Swimming at a motel, maybe. She only half–lied.

§

She's asleep when a thundering crack, a ferocious shudder, sends her hurtling from bed. Earthquake? The kids are crying in their room. She yells, "Get on the floor by the dresser. I'm coming," as she flies into the living room and trips, falling headfirst into something that shouldn't be here, something sharp scraping her face, something sharper stabbing her ribs. The smell of dust and dirt fill her nose. Then, the house isn't shaking at all. Cold air sweeps through her, and looking beyond the giant branches of a tree − a tree? − she sees a spray of stars. How did the night sky get inside her house?

The answer hits her. The oak from out front fell through the roof.

Collin wails, and Jamie, tangled up, can't get to her feet. She tears at her sweatpants caught on a broken branch. Grabs and yanks and yanks, but the fabric holds. Panic clogs her chest as she struggles to break free.

"Mama!" cries Collin.

"We can't get out," hollers Lily.

"I'm coming." Scratching, thrashing, cursing, Jamie drags off her pants, and leaving them dangling on a stem, she tries to climb into the living room, but a limb cracks under her weight. And where the hell is Sean? The fucker.

She struggles out of the jumble of wood and prickly leaves, and crawls into her bedroom, spies Sean's baseball bat and uses it to smash the window. Jumps back as glass shatters, and then, carelessly knocking away the shards, scrambles onto the dresser and tumbles into the chill. The wind stings her legs, waters her eyes. A man rounds the corner of the cabin. Sean! But it's not Sean. Stumbling to her feet, she shoves the man toward the window of the second bedroom. "My kids! Help me get them out."

§

When Jamie and the man carry Lily and Collin around to the front of the house, the neighbors, the persistent wind whipping hair and bathrobes, rush to greet them. Jamie gapes at the giant oak on its side, her cabin sheared down the middle, with chaos and debris on one side, her own personal still—life on the other.

A short while later, lit by candles and a kerosene lamp, tenants from the other cabins crowd the landlady's living room like flickering ghosts. The man who helped Jamie rescue the kids clears a space on the sofa, hands her a blanket to cover her legs. She lets her children settle on her lap, wincing from her cuts and scratches, feeling out of body, out of time. The blustering wind howls.

She turns to the man, "Who *are* you?"

Mr. German puts his hand on the man's shoulder. "This is my boy, Mars. Just came down from Frisco." To his dad, this middle—aged man is still a kid.

"Thanks for getting my little guys out, Mars. How – how bad is it?"

"Wind up to 90 miles an hour," says Sybil, wrapped in one of her Hawaiian print housecoats, bringing over a tray of instant coffees. She hands one to Jamie. Mars and his dad take cups and nodding, move away to join the other cabin tenants hovering around the windows.

"I guess you couldn't wait for me to put in a skylight in your cabin," says Sybil to Jamie. "Glad you're all right. Your husband's not home, I take it?"

"No, he's roofing in Fresno."

"A roofer who no longer has a roof! You have your phone, honey?"

Jamie shakes her head. The landlady hands her a cell. "How about some hot chocolate for the kids? Might as well drink the milk before it spoils. We may not have electric for hours."

"Thank you. They'd like that." She watches Sybil thread her way through the clutch of neighbors, then punches numbers into the cell, thinking Sean should be here instead of gone. Always gone. She wants him here now. She sputters into his voice mail, "Come home. A tree – we – just come home."

After Lily and Collin fall asleep on their mother's lap, Mars helps her carry them into Sybil's second bedroom.

"How old are these two?" he asks.

"Almost three and five."

"Nice kids."

"They are. Thanks again, Mars. We're lucky you were around."

As he leaves, Sybil tiptoes in with jeans for Jamie to put on. "Everybody's outside. Go on to sleep, honey."

But sleep is the last thing Jamie can do.


As the sun creeps up, the wind turns quiet. The ravaged neighborhood is littered with broken limbs, twisted Eugenias, piles of leaves. A splintered electric pole, its wires strewn about, the corner stop sign bent at 45 degrees, sirens in the distance announce apocalypse. Neighbors from up and down the Old Road mutter about the mess, the noise, and the miracle that no one's seriously hurt.

Exhausted, Jamie gapes at her own disaster. Mars moves next to her, startling her, says, "It's not so bad," but she shakes her head and picks her way around the ruined cabin to her bedroom window, Mars ambling behind. "Kids sleeping?"

"Sybil's feeding them Cheerios. I need my phone. Sean probably left me a message."

"I can climb in and get it for you."

"Thanks, but just give me a boost. I want to look around."

"So your husband," he says. "He's not here?"

"He'll be here."

Once inside, Jamie searches the bedroom floor for her cell.

"Got it?" Mars peers in the window.

"Yeah." She holds it up. She moves closer to the door to the living room.

"Any message?"

"Yes," she lies.

The old oak sprawls like some kind of fallen dragon. Light sifts through branches, dust motes laze on air, her suitcase, the Samsonite, squashed by the foliage.

# Indignation

## by Sally–Anne Macomber

**To:** Milton Flaxmill, Red Cow Publishing
**From:** Trudy Polaris
**Date:** January 20, 2014 1:21 p.m.
**Re:** My Book

Milton,

I was dismayed to see that once again, on the latest version of my new book *Nuclear Fission in the Pyrénées*, emailed to me only this morning, that the title does not include the two accents in *Pyrénées*.

I have lived with this project for three years and the two accents are integral to the book.

I can only conclude their non–inclusion is a sign that you do not take me or my work as a writer seriously.

I will not be publishing my book with you or Red Cow Publishing, and will be taking it elsewhere.

Trudy Polaris

Tuesday, 21ˢᵗ January 2014

# Thorns

## by Mandy Nicol

The screen door twangs shut behind me and a dozen flies. I heave the shopping bags into the kitchen. Put the milk, meat and marge in the fridge and leave the rest on the bench, including the fourteen cans of dog food for Peregrine. Mum watches from the dining room. I flick the switch on the kettle.

"Cuppa?" I ask.

"Oh yes, I'm parched."

I look out the window. Peregrine is lying under the thorny acacia. Dead to the world. Didn't welcome me home, doesn't notice the rabbits nibbling along the dam paddock fence. I stare at him until the kettle boils. He doesn't move. *Shit, maybe he is dead.* I glance at all the dog food I bought then knock on the window. Loudly.

"What is it?" asks Mum. "Is something there? What's the matter Nadia?" Her voice rises to that shrill pitch she's fond of.

Peregrine has his head up, ears cocked towards the house.

"It's all right," I say, "Just rabbits getting too close to the roses."

I wonder what Mum will call her next dog. She'll have to work hard to beat Peregrine. I pour boiling water into the teapot. Can't use teabags when she's watching, even though I've proved she can't tell the difference.

"Any mail?" she asks.

"I got an invite to Tom and Ellie's wedding."

"Nothing else? Nothing for me?"

"Err, no Mum, nothing else."

She slumps, but only for a moment, and I wait for it. I count in my head and get to four.

"Well it's perfectly understandable. That job has him moving around like a movie star and now he's in New York. Hong Kong, Dubai, and now New York. New York! Can you believe it?"

She smiles at the photos on the mantelpiece before trundling along. "Of course he's probably still settling in and getting to know his way around, meeting people, going to dinner parties, you know how popular he is. Well, he always was popular, even as a little tacker. Remember his twenty–first? I think everyone in town was here. I bet they have him doing those, what do they call it now, meet and greets? Yes he'd be doing a lot of that, he'd be very good at it … I'm sure he just, well, he probably hasn't had a minute to himself …"

I keep my mouth shut, pour out the tea and get the last of her birthday cake out of the fridge.

# A New Ned

## by Margaret Bingel

Wednesdays are the worst. Ned wrote this in bold, angry letters across his new calendar, barely used, just opened three weeks ago when he remembered that January is technically a brand—new month, and with it, you open your brand—new calendar and hang it on the wall.

The calendar, a standard 12—month with holidays and weekdays measured out, pictures droopy—eyed beagles wearing monocles and top hats nestled between their floppy ears. Ned thinks beagles are the most unfortunate dogs, and now forced to wear these distasteful props … He stares at the January picture of a puppy yawning in bed, wearing a red bow—tie. Why does my mother insist on getting me these sad—looking calendars, he wonders. Does she really think this makes life bearable in any serious kind of way? She needs to get a dog. Ned sighs, and, looking at the January page repeats his angry words in his head.

Wednesdays are just the stupidest, most wasteful days of the week, especially when your Tuesdays are really your Mondays, on the first three—day weekend you get right after Christmas. He raises his hand and tracing the letters with his index finger, pretends to write it all over again. Of course, this is why I just took the whole damn week off, he thinks, fingernails dragging across the week where he wrote, VACATION, in neat red letters.

It isn't that he doesn't like the calendars his mother gives him, he thinks, as he sits down at the table to his coffee, newspaper, and cooling toast, but Ned Billingsly is not excited about growing old. Today, he thinks, as he sips his coffee and pushes aside his newspaper, is the day I'll make time stop.

He drinks the last of his coffee and eats the last of his toast. He lives alone, but loves to sit by his window and watch the buzzing people scuttling off to their appointments, schools, jobs, lovers, restaurants, and football and basketball and hiking and bird−watching. His favorites are the cyclists (they move so fast, like they're cheating death) and children. Children are special because they haven't figured out time yet, still living with the idea that the Now That Is Going On is What Will Always Be. He believes in children, even if he doesn't believe in himself anymore.

Ned looks out his window, and sees a chatty woman herding a group of yellow−jacketed, glassy−eyed, cold, breathing dragon's breath in the chilly January air automatons. Most likely a new group of outreach youth, Ned thinks. Or teachers. Probably teachers, he shrugs while standing up and moving his dishes to the sink. He turns the hot water on. Rubbing a soapy washcloth over his plate, he thinks about what it's like to be happy. As long as I get my gun, I'll be happy, Ned thinks, placing his dripping plate into the dish rack.

My gun, and my bullets.

Done with the dishes, he looks outside the window one more time. It's January, but the snow on the ground isn't so much light, fluffy stuff but deceiving ice piles and slicks on the sidewalks. The last thing Ned needs is to trip and hurt himself with his gun in his hand. He slips his coat on, and, feeling for his wallet and keys in his coat pockets, and looking down to check he has both shoes on his feet, he steps out into the cold, locks the door behind him, and walks towards the bus stop.

He walks past many beautiful things, things he's seeing for the first time: trees with snow−covered branches; prismatic icicles; two women in love, strolling and laughing, their mittened hands clasped together. While watching the beautiful women, he doesn't see the patch of black ice on the sidewalk. Stepping on it, his leather soles slip out from under him, and he falls backwards, his head smacking pavement.

One of the women breaks her clasp and rushes towards him.

Ned doesn't respond. With his eyes half-closed, he looks like he's dreaming. Blood leaks from his ears, and falls in droplets on the ice.

Thursday, 23rd January 2014

# I was a fool yesterday

## by Darryl Price

I was a fool yesterday. I'm still a fool today. I can feel it in my bones. Sleep did nothing to dampen this sensation in me. Does this feel good? I'm not really so sure. Yesterday it felt like I had discovered something so right that it just might change the world as we know it. Today I only know I am still in the full grip of this thing that renders me useless to myself as a trained to take a bullet for the King bodyguard. I have become a second–class citizen in my own country of self. How is this even possible you ask? Well, let me start by saying that sometimes we are very simply confronted out of the blue with someone so beautiful that we become instantly obsolete ourselves from the brush of experience. It wipes us out, and when we do discover we may still have say certain rudimentary motor skills such as walking and talking they become a wonder to us, as if newly procured. That's what I'm trying to tell you. This has happened to me. And today I mean to act upon it – if I can get out of bed and showered in time to again meet my destiny face to face and ask her out. But I'm not done telling you about this phenomenon yet. Here, let me start it all over again for you. It's fun. Or crazy. And. I want to. It's that fantastic! Just like in the movies you feel like making a kooky song out of anything that moves, anything mundane. The sun through the stupid blue curtains. All of a sudden like a stage full of soft ballerinas dancing in unison to a low slow moon song. The way your slippers feel sliding onto your feet first thing. An excited bird tattling on a bad cat outside the still drying off from the clouds of night early morning window. The click of the same lamp switch becomes a bittersweet call to arm. A car going by and fading into another lost silence. All incredible. I mean it. Anything becomes everything. You can't help but make that connection from now on. It's impossible and happening and you feel hungry and full at the same time. The water coming out of the faucet is nothing short of an actual bona fide miracle. Do you get the picture? The man in the mirror is for real. Dude. It's all too much. And you can never get enough. Never never never.

# People Skills

## by Teresa Burns Gunther

I can hear Stella halfway down the block. As soon as my key's in the lock she's at the door. Stella's long legged and sleek. All I want to do is rip off my suit and dive into a cold drink – it's been a shitty day. I didn't get my raise; my boss says I need to work on my people skills. He'll find any excuse. Last time it was presentation skills. What next? Better Post−it note placement?

"All right Stella. Hold your horses." She's all over me, slobbering love, then sniffing my heels after I kick them off. I'm so happy to see her. She goes bat shit as I slip on clogs and grab her leash. She drags me out of the house barking at anything that moves. I pull my coat closed against the wind. Joyce and Larry are out front. Stella jerks her leash from my hand and races up their walk, growling. Joyce double−times it up her stairs.

"Stella! No!" I hurry to grab her leash.

"She's a ticking toim bomb," Joyce says in her hard−edged Australian. She glares down on us from her top step, arms crossed on her massive breasts. "You should muzzle that beast." You'd guess she's a dyke by her buzz cut and baggy clothes, but she's married. To Larry, a software engineer complete with long, pale ponytail, thick glasses and teeth so crooked it hurts to look at them. Larry stands like a string bean wall between Joyce and Stella, his arms spread wide for protection.

"She wouldn't hurt a flea," I say, coiling Stella's leash and holding her close. "You just don't know her."

Joyce's shoulders are up in her ears like she expects Stella to shred her porcine body. Stella's a beauty; a mix of Akita, Shepherd and Ridgeback; at least that's what the vet and I figure. She's the sweetest dog in the world, a little territorial, but as a single woman in San Francisco I like that she's watching my back. People these days … if they aren't crazy, they're just plain nuts. I get that some people are afraid of dogs; they say they have good reasons, but in my opinion they're missing an important chromosome in their DNA. Stella's the only person I can count on.

"She's just wound up," I tell Larry. "She needs her walk. TGIF."

"Hey," Larry calls after us. "We're having friends round later if you'd like to come by." Joyce looks like she might bite him. I say thanks, but no, I have a hot date.

I do have a date, through an internet service. I always thought dating services were for losers, but it's not something I'm good at. Because, I'm not a phony. I hate pretending to like someone or fake interest when I don't feel it.

When my doorbell rings I lock Stella in the kitchen. I'm disappointed when I open the door. Another fool who lies about his height. Do guys really think I won't notice?

"Hi, Rachel?"

I nod.

"I'm Bart."

I sigh. "Clearly, you're a creative writer."

"Pardon," he says, his shaggy head tilted.

"You said you were 5'11"." I open the door. "Come in."

He hesitates, looks back at the street, then steps inside. "Nice place," he says.

"Thank you." I close the door. "Want a drink. I sure could use one." I remember I'm working on my people skills. "Do you like wine, beer, or tequila?" I smile.

"A beer sounds good." His voice is loud and Stella starts barking. Bart eyes the kitchen door, shaking as she fights to get out.

"I hope you like dogs."

"Oh, yeah," he says, weakly. The five o'clock shadow on his round face is not a good look.

I grab Stella by the collar and bring her out. "Stella, this is Bart." I laugh at the way the fur rises up along her spine. She's so cute. "Meet my bodyguard."

"Jesus," Bart says, inching away. "She looks like she's out for blood."

I put Stella in my bedroom and tell her Bart's a scaredy–cat but no way will he try any funny business. She barks when I close the door. "Quiet Stella." She sniffs and I hear her jump up on my bed.

"Hey," Bart says, standing by the door, "Wanna go out? I saw a place down the street."

Outside, it's a clear night, though cold without a fog blanket. I'm relieved to see Mrs. Franklin has finally taken down her Christmas decorations. All that fake joy irritates me.

"How about pizza and beer?" Bart says. "I'm starved."

I want to say that it wouldn't hurt him to miss a meal, but stop myself, because I *do* have people skills. We go to Firavanti's, a mediocre place I'm tired of. But the flats I put on for Bart pinch my feet and clearly this guy isn't springing for a taxi.

We order, then do the *where are you froms?* and family histories, though mine is short. It's just me now, if you don't count a cousin always looking for a handout and a theatrical father who lives for a stage unless it's a family home. He exited stage left from ours when I was six.

"Has your dog ever bitten anyone?" he asks.

"You're afraid?"

"Hell ya. He looks hungry." He grins.

"Stella's a she."

His smile drops, but picks back up a little when the beer arrives.

"So what do you do?" he asks. I see him check his watch.

"I take money from dead people."

"Come again?" he asks.

"I work for the IRS. Probate." He starts to say something, but I hold up my hand. "Believe me, I've heard every IRS sob story there is." He purses his lips. That's when the pizza arrives.

We eat for a few minutes. Things are going pretty well. I ask him about his work. He smiles. "I teach political science at the university."

"That must be hard," I say.

"Sometimes." He nods. "I like it," he says. "It's a great job. The kids are pretty smart. It's exciting to see young people get involved in the world, developing their own opinions now that they're out from under the dominance of their parents' ideas." He smiles. "It's my opinion that −"

"You know what they say about opinions? They're like assholes, everybody has one." It cracks me up. I slap the table. Someone told me that once. Hysterical. But I'm laughing alone. "Don't you think that's funny?"

"What? Calling me an asshole?"

"It's a *joke*. Wow, you're sensitive."

He watches me while he eats, then asks, "Have you been on many dates − with lovematch.com?"

"Yeah. They've all been pretty bad. How about you?"

He raises his eyebrows. "Some," he says, "are better than others. Much better."

"Isn't that the truth?" I say. "And my boss thinks I need to work on my people skills." I shake my head. "Can you believe that?"

He nods like the professor he claims to be and says, "Sage advice." Then he signals the waiter and asks her to split the bill.

Saturday, 25<sup>th</sup> January 2014

# Morgana Malone and the Case of the Mysterious Flood

## by Matt Potter

"You have no idea what you're talking about, do you?"

He's at it again. With five minutes of the gallery tour left, his voice still sounds from the rear of the twenty—plus group: soft enough for the old ladies in front not to hear, but insistent enough that I wait for his intake of breath before he speaks, and wince.

And I was hoping my new orange bob made me unrecognisable.

"You can see by the way the colours *pop* out at your eyes," I say, hand shaking at the picture throbbing on the wall, my apricot broderie Anglaise shoulder ruffle flapping against my upper arm. "It's a really eye—popping painting." I turn my head from the blue and yellow and green and purple and other ugly colour swirls and step towards the doorway.

"Nobody has any idea what she's saying," he says — to someone, anyone, no one, everyone, who knows: the old ladies have all turned away from him as far as I can tell. "She's talking into the ether and it sounds like Sanskrit. And that hair colour?" he snorts. "She looks like a carrot."

My heels clack on the parquet floor as I walk, through the large doorway and into the next gallery. I'd challenge him, if this wasn't my first day on the job. *Carrots used to be your favourite vegetable*, I'd say. And wait for him to deny it.

Perhaps becoming a volunteer gallery guide to meet men was not such a good idea.

(I'm so sick of bogus profiles on the internet! They all look great on the screen — *Me: down to earth, like people to be themselves, good sense of humour* — but then you meet them! Men worth millions still living with their mothers. Men who are 'single' betrayed by their wedding ring tan lines. Men who say, "I'm paying so much in child support I need to know how fertile you are," even before I buy them a drink.)

I clasp my hands in front of me as I turn on my high heels to face the group. Two old ladies stare, giving me their brightest attention.

"As you can see by the brilliant bas−reliefs above us on the ceiling, we're now in the original part of the Gallery." I clasp my hands tighter, to stop myself from gesturing towards the ceiling with shaky fingers, to keep my balance on my high heels.

Old ladies muster around me.

A guffaw sounds from the back of the group.

The bastard knows I've always hated my brown hair.

"This part of the Gallery first opened in 1882," I say, "and was built with a generous bequest from Sir Farquhar McPherson, whose brother Sir Darymple McPherson made an equally generous bequest three years later, to match the original."

"What media were used to create the bas−reliefs?" He's standing off to the side now.

I look at him and see there's something different about his eyes: whitened, and flattened, like the wrinkles have been blasted off.

"They look incredibly unique," he adds, "or maybe even uniquely incredible, so I'm fascinated to know what they're made of." He smiles. "Can you inform us?"

I look at another older woman who stands, head cocked, waiting for my answer. A gold tooth glints inside her puckering mouth.

"Plaster of Paris, creek water and old egg cartons," I say, "all mooshed together in a big cauldron and slapped up there with large paintbrushes made of virgin horsehair." I smile, holding back a scream. "Thanks for joining me on this tour this afternoon. Please enjoy the rest of the Gallery."

I turn. My heels are brisk on the marble floor and as I pass him I smell his cologne, woodsy in that Eastern Bloc way I remember so well. "Don't follow me, Grigor," I say, "or I'll call Security."

Other voices disappear behind me. I walk through the next doorway, head down, heels clacking, and then through another door and then another door marked 'Staff Only' and down the stairs, clack−clacking my way to the toilets marked 'DANGER − subject to flooding'.

As soon as I hear the restroom door pushing open, my eyes flash to the latch. Unless he climbs over or under the cubicle walls or over or under the door or has a screwdriver to unscrew the lock or a gun to shoot the lock off, I'm safe sitting on the toilet lid.

The restroom door wheezes closed behind him. Knuckles rap hard on the cubicle door.

I hold my breath.

"What are you doing, Morgana? Why are you pretending to be someone you're not? As soon as I walked into the gallery and saw you standing by the *Guided Tours here* sign with your shoulders slouched and hugging your elbows like a street waif, I knew it was you. You can't hide behind that orange hair colour."

My eyes are wild in my head. "You have no right to come here, Grigor. This is for staff only." I answer with what I hope is strength and confidence.

*But you're not staff, you're only a volunteer,* I expect him to say.

"Your voice sounds weak and unconfident," he says instead. His signature Spanish sandals poke under the door and his voice sounds skewed, as if he's talking into the painted wood and his chest. "You need to come back to intensive therapy."

I look down at my shoes. Open−toed and two−tone peach and tangerine to match my hair, they're a mere school ruler−length away from touching the toes of Grigor's sandals and perfect for a January summer day except the closed heels rub raw under my ankle bones and they're so high any degree of nerves makes the balancing act −

"I have a free appointment at 9.30 on Monday," he says. "I can get Zebadie to block the time out in my schedule for you. I can call her now and get her to keep it free. I can do that if you want, Morgana." He shifts his weight and his sandals squeak on the marble floor. "I can do that for you right now. I can call her up and tell her it's an emergency and have you booked in for 9.30 Monday morning. It's as easy as that." I hear the rustling of fabric. "I'm getting my mobile out of my pocket now and calling Zebadie to make the appointment, even though it's a Saturday now. And you won't have to do anything but turn up at 9.30 on Monday. That's only two days away."

I clear my throat. "I won't marry you to get discount therapy, Grigor."

"You won't have to this time," he sighs.

I shake my head.

His voice softens. "Things will be different this time."

I fold my hands in my lap. I have another thirty minutes before my next tour and after fifteen years in therapy with poor timekeepers, am pretty good at waiting.

"Please," he says.

I twiddle my thumbs, then breathe out, relaxing my spine and slouching against the cistern, my apricot broderie Anglaise shoulder ruffle now reaching down to my navel.

"I promise," he whispers.

I can't believe I say it, but I do. "What did you do to your eyes, Grigor?"

I hear a sharp intake of breath against the door. I wince.

"Just some light freshening up," he says. "They help me see better into people's psyches now the excess skinfolds are gone, so I have a much clearer vision and I'm really pleased with the result. Now my eyes look the way they were always meant to look."

I remember the mirror he kept behind the couch in his consulting room. He would watch his reflection while counselling patients about their body image problems.

Grigor's voice deepens again. "But that's really not important now, Morgana. It hasn't escaped my notice that you've dyed your hair the colour of my favourite vegetable."

I cross my ankles, but leaning back perched on the toilet lid with crossed ankles doesn't work (unless I want to stretch out and touch toe–to–toe with Grigor) so put my hands by my side, wrapping my fingers around the edge of the seat to steady myself. But the cold of the white porcelain is a shock to my fingertips so I sit up again. The toilet seat creaks.

"Are you constipated, Morgana?"

Standing up, I press the button. The sound of water splashing out of the cistern and into the bowl fills the cubicle. And then I feel wet washing past my toes, and looking down see water rushing from behind the bowl and flooding across the marble. "Oh," I say.

Grigor's Spanish sandals step backward and I hear wet splotching across the floor. "I'll get Security," he says, and the door opens and wheezes closed.

Pressing the button again, I watch more water flood across the floor. "Call Emergency Services too!" I shout, hoping he hears. Cistern half full and I press it again.

I bought a *Men of Emergency Services* calendar last week and a lot of those guys look definitely single.

# Breakable

## by Gary Percesepe

Yesterday morning I moved my just–divorced self into a new house. In the afternoon I went to the dentist.

A root canal tooth was acting up. I need a new crown. $500 after insurance. My ex is a teacher, with excellent insurance and small co–pays. The day we signed divorce papers, barely a month ago, I lost my health care coverage and had to COBRA.

This morning I woke in the old house and realized I had no clothes. I did have the dog of the family. Dylan spent the night with me at the old house. My ex is spending the summer with her new boyfriend in another state. I think it is Arkansas, but it might be Missouri. I get those two confused. She asked me, could I watch the dog while she is gone? I said sure.

But I had taken my summer clothes over to the new house. So, no clothes. Also, no shoes. They were in a Hefty trash bag, my shorts and tops in another. I moved them in the fourteen foot U–Haul truck that a friend rented for me. I threw the two Hefty bags on the floor of the closet in the guest room at the new house.

The landlord at the new house says no dogs. So I spent the night at the old house with the dog, but without clean underwear or a change of clothes. Also missing were some books I've been reading, books that I keep stacked on the end table next to my bed, along with my writer's journal, in which I scribble story ideas, bits of poems, memories from childhood, impressions from the day. Movie scenes with notes: *Kate Beckinsale running, tight T, face pinched, write story from mood.* The bed and the books are at the new house, three miles across town. Along with the journal. The dog of the family looks at me and yawns.

I put on yesterday's clothes and go to the new house.

On the drive over I think about a woman I know in New York. Pari is getting a divorce. She is a writer, too. A damn good one. I would say she's "in the middle of a divorce" but it's hard to know if she's in the middle, since it feels like this will go on forever, and what's half of forever? Her ex is a Wall Street guy who moved his girlfriend into the country house in Connecticut that Pari decorated, even as Pari was having to move into her mother's basement in Jersey.

The other day, Pari took her two kids by taxi to Penn Station. She texted me to say that they were headed to the Hamptons to stay with a friend for a few days. Eliot is twenty months, her brother Sawyer is five. The three of them got on the train and Pari texted me again. Elie was singing the ABC song, but all she knew was, *"Now I know my."* Just that much, *"Now I know my,"* over and over in her baby voice. "She calls Sawyer *Waya* and herself *It*," P texted. "My two kids, Waya and It."

I'm a native New Yorker, living in exile in Ohio for many years but returning about once a month to see family, visit with friends, and occasionally give readings from my novel. I'm considerably older than Pari. We met on an online dating service. At the start, we agreed to take romance off the table.

That worked for a while. We said: friends, sure. We lived in different states.

Soon enough we were talking on the phone. Texts and emails. Things speeded up. We shared comical stories of dates gone bad, of how unfit we were for human relationship.

Then one night, walking back to her place in Tribeca after a reading, she gave me a sidelong glance. A sly smile, and then she jumped at me. Mid air, I caught her, and we stumbled back off the sidewalk of West 4<sup>th</sup> Street to the side of the Hebrew Union. She is Jewish. We laughed at that, and collapsed in a heap against the cold brick wall, pulling at each other's clothes.

A month later we were in a hotel room. It wasn't so much that we fooled around. It was that we'd laughed and cried together. We told each other things we'd told no one in this world. Beating her small fists into the hotel pillow, she curled into a fetal position and asked me to hold her. These are things difficult to forget.

Sometimes I feel like a barometer. I register every feeling in the forest. I would like to feel less.

When I am with women other than Pari, however, I feel nothing. Even when having sex. OK, when having lots of sex. Nothing.

One morning, before we had met face to face, she sent me an email from her BlackBerry. "I've a half gallon of whole milk in my arm like a baguette. Such is life with two wee adorable mongrels. Milk and strawberries and goldfish crackers. Three meals a day of this. Better than tying cooking twine around roasts for a grumpy banker who says too salty or worse I'm not hungry. I'm sad, Gary. Angry often but deeper, sad."

Sometimes I wonder if Pari is a place holder for me, holding the place I have reserved for love once I am able to feel again. Love is so easy to mimic, especially for writers. Sometimes I worry that, having met her, and felt the deep connection we have felt, having cried together, with the memory of her runner's body quivering in my arms, her tiny starfish hands, her size five feet that I bought shoes for in Italy and handed to her in the lobby of her building in New York, to cries of delight – oh, we're not in love. We are divorce friends, fellow travelers. But I *could* have loved her. I wonder if I will ever be able to love anyone ever again in the way that I have loved Pari. She is impossible for me, an impossible love, but by loving her I keep at a distance all possible loves. She is safe and unsafe at the same time. She holds the place where I hope to show up again, missing less.

We both feel something, maybe even something like love, but there's nothing to be done about it.

The furniture I moved to the new house looks comical in its new setting. The old house is an Italianate beauty, over 5,000 square feet, with twenty rooms. A winding mahogany staircase built in 1860 that looks like it was borrowed from the set of *Gone With the Wind*. Large paintings that had been hung with care on walls twelve foot high.

The new place is an 800 square foot box. Two small bedrooms. The master bedroom is barely large enough to contain my king—sized bed and dresser. If Gulliver had furniture it would have looked something like this.

I go to the guest room to retrieve the two Hefty bags. Then I go out to the garage and locate the box that holds my bed books. I sort through the box until I locate the books I need: three books by James Salter, a novel by Meg Wolitzer, the new translation of Proust by Lydia Davis, and two memoirs by Dani Shapiro that I have been re—reading as I prepare to interview her.

It's Sunday. I look at my watch. A day to kill. Kill the days. My new vocation. I decide to drive to Yellow Springs to see a movie. Something about sitting alone in a dark room appeals to me. A way to escape, sure, though I'm perfectly aware that it is me I am trying to escape. Stories help. Anyone's story. Anyone but me. A place to give myself the slip. Isn't this the purpose of movies? But looking for a parking space in town, I find myself thinking about my visit to the dentist yesterday. And the girl who worked on me.

Open wider, she'd said. We've got to get this old glue off.

She held her silver instrument tight in her gloved hand. Into the maw of me, this pink cavity, past my confused tongue, the family voice thick in my throat, she probed deeper.

I wondered if she was pissed because she had to come in to work on a Saturday, but didn't have much time for that thought. I flinched.

It's a root canal tooth so you shouldn't feel any pain. Except when I get below the gum.

I squirmed. Gripped the arm of the chair tighter.

Are you OK? We can get you some Novocain.

I'm fine.

I told you to watch what you eat. What did you eat for breakfast this morning?

Granola, I said.

Uh huh, she said. In her goggles and her 1980s Stevie Nicks hair she looked like bad MTV.

Sorry. What should I be eating?

Soup. Yogurt. Soft stuff. It's on the paper I gave you.

I threw it away by mistake.

It's OK, Stevie said. The other option is, you can keep coming in here every day for a new cap.

Thanks.

She told me the dentist waived the $500. Somehow he must have gotten the news about me. Is it that obvious? In the same way that a friend paid for the U—Haul yesterday, and four of my friends spent a half—day moving me. Jeff and Richele disassembled my bed. I couldn't bear to watch. They re—assembled it at the new house. I shut the door. Later, I hugged them.

Most of the time I feel like a rambling wreck, but there are occasional grace notes. The way that Pari cares about me, and that I care about her, even though we cannot use the L word, even though we are not "in love", even though we both know it's not us. But we can still accompany each other. Even when it appears we walk in circles in the dark, we're together, somehow, through this. That's grace, too.

The assistant discarded her goggles and turned off the bright light she'd trained on me. She looked less like a space alien this way.

Look at it this way, she said. You've got a thin piece of plastic in your mouth. It's a temporary plastic crown. You have to be careful, OK? It's breakable.

The village is crowded. Dinner, movies. Couples. Shapes, sizes, colors, genders. Some holding hands. Some not.

Miraculously, a space opens in front of Mr. Fub's Party. Where I'd purchased so many toys for my kids when they were small. Grown now. No more toys.

I back into the space, thinking of Stevie. Breakable, she'd said. I know what she means.

# Waking Up Samford

## by Nathaniel Tower

Samford McGee wakes in a sweat. "What day is it?" he asks the naked woman at his side. He has no idea what her name is or where she came from or if she is even a woman at all. It might be a waxed man with long hair. Or perhaps a mannequin. Or maybe even an alien life form.

The body turns to look at him and smiles. It's a living thing, that's for sure. Definitely a woman. Look at those cheek bones. No man could look like that.

"It's Monday, silly," she coos as she cranes in for a kiss. Her breath reeks of cheap booze.

"No, what's the date," he says.

"January 27<sup>th</sup>," she says, her breath more foul than before, as if the second opening of her cavern has released the full power of the stench.

"No, I don't think that's right," another voice says, and Samford suddenly realizes there's someone else in bed with them. He props himself up on his elbows and peers over the woman's body, scanning her for hideous flaws in the process. He finds none and relaxes momentarily until he notices the body on the other side is not another woman.

"It's definitely the 27<sup>th</sup>," the woman says, her finger sliding across her phone. "See? Says it right here."

Samford wonders how she managed to conjure the phone. He scans her body for a secret compartment, but the only openings he sees don't look big enough. As she pulverizes the phone screen with her fingertips using impossible rapidity, Samford peeks at the creature on her other side. The man is hideous, but Samford can't stop looking. He knows this man from somewhere, he's certain of it. The idea that they have slept together, in the carnal sense that is, creeps into Samford's mind and he turns his eyes back to the woman. Her flawless body tells him he would have done anything she had told him.

Samford drops flat on the mattress, the impact rippling under the other bodies. Both stir, but neither looks at him. A rickety coil springs into Samford's back, and he shifts to find some comfort.

When the woman takes a break from her all–important phone messaging, he taps her shoulder and, leaning in close, whispers, "Who is that?" He even points, as if the question itself isn't obvious enough.

She laughs but says nothing.

"What the hell's so funny?" He's still close to her ear, and she recoils at the boom of his yell. The other man props himself up and glares at Samford.

Shaking her head free of the ringing, she laughs again. "You really don't know who this is?" She looks over at the man and they share a laugh. The man slaps her thigh and Samford watches the skin and tissue jiggle up and down her leg.

"No, I don't. Look, I don't know what spell you have used on me, but I want answers!" Samford roars. She must be some type of witch. He sits up fully, tugging the sheet to cover his shriveled member. His eyes drift down for comparison, and he sees the other man's member is just as shriveled.

"Relax," she says as she brushes her fingertips along the sheets covering his thigh, eliciting instant erection. Samford is unsure why, but the other man is suddenly erect as well.

"Tell me the truth!" he yells. He's staring at the other man this time, and the answer starts to make itself clear to him. The woman confirms it.

"Why, he's you, silly." She laughs again, as does the man.

Samford doesn't quite understand, but he doesn't need to ask. The woman hands him a brochure. Again, he is unsure how she summoned this item.

Samford scans the brochure and it all makes sense.

"So you cloned me?"

"Something like that."

How does he know if he is the real Samford? Perhaps the woman brought the other man home, engaged in raging intercourse with him, then created the body that the man who currently believes is the real Samford is currently residing in. He doesn't know for sure that any raging intercourse has been had. He just assumes that any man naked with her must have done something. The clouds in his mind make him almost certain that he isn't the real Samford. The real Samford would remember a night like that.

Samford, or the man who believes he might not be the real Samford anymore, leaps out of bed, his erect member bouncing like a jack–in–the–box. Pointing a finger, he shouts, "I want him out of my house." As he stares at the man, he decides that *he* isn't the real Samford either.

"It's my house," the man says.

Samford looks around and does not recognize a single thing here. For a moment, he stares at the couple, naked on the bed that isn't his. His body begins shaking and he points his finger at the giggling pair. "I refuse to stand idly by and be a clone of an ugly man!" he roars at them before bolting from the room, tears flooding his eyes. He hears erupting laughter and the sudden sounds of spontaneous lovemaking. Covering his ears, doors banging behind him, he sprints down the street. Even with his hands above his head, the smacking of his feet on the pavement and the slapping of his erection against his legs is deafening. He will run until he's home, but then … he has no idea if he has any real home at all.

Tuesday, 28<sup>th</sup> January 2014

# Twelve Days Old

## by Kimberlee Smith

Etheline Margaret Pritchett, my baby, latches onto the handmade rattle dangling from her daddy Dean's fingertips with a purity of instinct and fervor as if she's reaching out to my breast for the first time. She wraps her sweet, plump fist around the circle of cloudy yellow ribbed spires, each nub as long as a dog's fang. Her bare feet pump in the air and her arms flail with the spontaneous reaction to thousands of nerves awakening. She looks up to Dean and my mum Maybell's faces glowing down upon her. I'm glowing on her, too.

You'd never reckon they've just come home from the funeral except that Dean is wearing a brand–new black suit and Maybell is in her Sunday church dress, thick black hose, and some fancy black shoes that maybe even came from that posh department store David Jones.

They stopped on the way home from the cemetery at Doyle's for fish and chips and watched the blinding white cruise ships docked at Circular Quay, seeing that Dean's parents had never been there and this is a special day. They'd driven up from Jervis Bay for the service and lunch, but are tear–assing right back down, not even staying long enough to pay a visit to our new house. I feel like its mine, still.

Today Etheline is twelve days old. I'm her mum, Melodie Margaret Pritchett, and I'm twelve days dead. Today was my funeral.

I watch, as I have since the day I was bitten by that coral snake, but as time passes the urge to remain so close to them weakens. Now, that transition might seem selfish or insensitive, but unless you've died you can't imagine how things tweak and your mind isn't your same mind, seeing things differently than when I was in my body, alive. Bear with me now, because I am new to this whole death thing. And not that I knew what to expect; in truth, I never gave it a thought, my own death. But here it is.

Before I get into what's going on today, January 28 (one of the hottest days of the summer, it seems, with water restrictions and panting dogs and nothing much moving at all) I'll let you know that it's pissing me off how everyone's sitting around the table during tea discussing my own personal afterlife.

Maybell's mewing like a newborn kitten that can't latch on to a teat. She's certain I found everlasting peace and that God's hanging around making sure every wish I ever had is coming true. Dean and his parents sit there mute, nodding like those hard plastic bobble−headed figurines. I try to box his mum Doreen's ears − I know she never cared for me back then or even now − but my damn hands passed right through her head like a vapour and my arms just wrapped around myself and passed through me as well.

The theory that I'm in *Heaven,* like it's a place you fly up to in First Class or something, is what they're comforting each other with in conversation. But it's just an abstract something that people conjure up when a loved one dies. A fable for the living so they don't have to think about what might be the truth, and I'll tell you, it is. That when you die, you're just *gone.*

As of yet, I've not travelled through a tunnel of light and butterflies, passed through pearly gates, danced on a moonbeam, or floated on a cloud. No harps, no angels. No nothing. All that romantic, gooey stuff is supposed to happen right away, from what I was led to believe as a child. No reuniting with long-gone relatives or old beloved pets. What a fucking downer.

I think I'm still here in their world, somewhere. I feel lost. What my family considers the passing of time is a measure of distance; time has no purpose here. Everything happens in what could be a second or even an eternity. I am afraid I'm slipping fluidly away. I don't have a supernatural skill set that I can use to flap the feathery white wings I'm kind of waiting for – would be nice; a gift upon arrival – to say where or how I go anywhere from here, wherever here is.

I find my *self* (the abstract part, not the body part) in this limbo land and the sensation is like I'm looking in a rearview mirror. Some distance, some hindsight, and a heap of uselessness. Retrospection and hindsight are gifts that deliver wisdom to the living. But since the dead don't grow, I haven't figured out how to put them to any practical use. Other than to tell you about Etheline in a way no one else can, the way I'm experiencing it. So stay with me.


Only two months have passed since we moved into our house at Kookaburra Springs outside of Homebush. On the way home from Doyle's, Maybell and Dean lament that it would have been much kinder on all of us if they didn't have to wait so long to get my body into the ground. *Tests* had to be run. They didn't argue, probably out of guilt. I should hope so, anyway, on account of the accident mainly because they keep the serpents *in the house*. But I'll get into that later. I've got nowhere to go, and you might as well be patient and hang on. It's a mindblower of an accident, my death. I'm not quite comfortable explaining the circumstances of it, not quite yet. I can barely believe it, myself.

My family watched the cemetery workers (maybe they were the gravediggers, too, but they must've tidied themselves up a bit) lower my good old wooden casket – my physical *forever home* – two meters deep in a hole dug out of the dirt especially for yours truly this morning just as the scorching fireball that is our closest star hauled itself up from the western horizon into the sky. Flies were droning drunkenly, aimlessly. Thousands of despondent jacaranda blossoms surrendered to the brutality of the day … it's important to note that jacaranda trees have always been my favourite, and oh, oh, especially at that magic hour when the sun needs to be dragged to bed and the floral perfume just about screams out to you.

For Christmas, just a month and three days ago, as a gift to me and to celebrate our new home, Dean planted a half dozen baby jacaranda trees in the front garden of our house. It was a really great surprise. He told me he got up as soon as I had fallen asleep that Christmas Eve and was digging, planting, and watering the infantile trees until sunrise. Man oh man, was he proud of himself for keeping such a secret. Maybell didn't even know. He said he was nervous as a bug they were going to die, since he had them hidden for two days in our shed. Kept checking on them and making sure they didn't dry out, their tiny root balls wrapped in burlap sacks. He tended to them every day. He would sing quietly as he cared for them, but I teased him he wasn't singing to himself, he was singing to the jacarandas. Now he tends to them with an obsession as if I myself had reincarnated those saplings. And I know when he sings, he's singing to me.

§

When he and Maybell brought our baby home from hospital, he stood in the front garden for what must have been an hour, crying his eyes out. It hit him right then that I would never get to enjoy those trees, but in a strange and kind of beautiful twist of fate, Etheline Margaret would be able do so with him. He promised her and himself (and even Maybell, who lives with us) through choked sobs and a broken bird voice that he would tell her the story of Melodie's Christmas trees to our baby girl as a tradition, every Christmas Eve. It's a sweet thought, but maybe a wee bit depressing when the baby starts to grow into a little girl and gets crazy excited about Father Christmas coming but all her daddy wants to talk about is dead mum's trees. I hope that's a temporary, stage–of–grieving type of thing.

So back at the cemetery, poor Dean soaked through his suit, but holy smokes did he look handsome as the day I met him ten years ago, and Mum's armpits had sweat rings the size of melons staining them. I bet she would have plucked out her own eyeball to take off those rubbery black hose. Even in that atrocious 38°C heat, Dean cupped his hand around Mum's shoulder to steady her, taking care not to squeeze her into him too hard, but I know he needed it, too.

My corpse was like a puckered old balloon that lost its helium, gussied up in one of Maybell's formalish dinner dresses – the only thing that fit on account of my abdomen is still stretched out from the baby. The man at the funeral home says my regular clothes won't fit right (I don't know if he meant he couldn't squeeze me into them, or for some insane reason they might appear uncomfortable at the viewing?) even though the baby was born nearly two weeks ago. Reason being it takes a while for the maternal swelling to go down, even though they drained out the bodily fluids that pooled on account of gravity. I'm a postmortem paperweight, if you need help visualizing this nightmare. Maybell has them dress me up just like her, though I'm sixteen years younger. So the mortician made me look half−whore, half−marionette. I don't wear makeup, never have. What a travesty.

They had some help from the hospital trying to locate my father to let him know a granddaughter was born and also that at that same time his own daughter passed away. He was long gone, on a traveling revival, spreading the word of his precious Bible, and he could not be found. It's just as well.

On this twelfth day, Etheline's wrist twitches and a jagged rattle spire grazes her cheek. Her mouth flies wide open and her eyes clench shut like there's fire in them and she howls one prolonged, plaintive wail that fades like a dying spark. A thin trickle of blood dribbles down her face from the duct of her left eye to the crease at her left nostril, then down the peachy little slope that reaches her top lip. Her eyes are amber slits. Like a serpent's. She slips a few of the rattle spires between her lips and suckles and the blood from the tear of her skin makes her lips the color of cherry cordial.

"Well *GOD* damn! She scratched herself up pretty good, but it don't seem to faze her. Smiling, she is, even! Tough as nails, just like her mum," Dean says.

Maybell speed walks from the family room where they keep the Moses basket that Etheline sleeps in over to the kitchen sink, wets a bleached rag with cold water from the tap and just about runs back to the baby, daubs the track of blood that trails down Etheline's face, then presses the rag tenderly against the wound to stop the blood from coming.

"Oh, shut up with that nonsense. And don't take the Lord's name in vain, will you not, *please!*" Maybell says all squinty−eyed and sour−pussy. "That there is just gas looking like a smile. And the baby did not scratch herself up, your toy did. It's dangerous as the snake itself. Reminds me in a bad way of Melodie. A real bad one."

She'll be scarred for life, I'm certain. But the weird thing is, instead of losing color from the trauma, her face flushes like a porcelain doll with dollops of rouge on her cheeks. The cut triggers something that makes her even more vibrant and alive. I am not entirely surprised. Our family has a long history with incidents of unusual sorts.

By now Dean's out on the front porch smoking a cigarette he just rolled for himself. He likes the tobacco that smells like cloves. He sucks in hard and exhales deep to keep breathing steady and stifling the complicated thoughts swirling around in his head like a tornado, else he might find himself saying something that'll bite him in the ass.

"Do you mind? That smoke is blowing back through the screen and stinking up the whole house," Maybell says. "Terrible for the baby, second−hand smoke. You know I been trying to quit. A little consideration wouldn't hurt." I have to agree.

Dean crushes the sweet and pungent butt out in a ceramic ashtray shaped like a saltwater crocodile. Gold script across its scales spells out 'February 14, 2012 Dean + Melodie 4 ∞'. We had the inscription done custom. It was a souvenir from our wedding up on the Sunshine Coast. I think that's all we got in terms of keepsakes.

So, I wonder now. *Infinity.* ∞.

# Slim Jim

## by Vanessa Weibler Paris

I always wanted to go by Jamie, but by the time I was old enough to say so, there was no escaping it: I was Slim Jim.

In reality, it doesn't matter what I'd been named: The kids — and later, the adults — would find a way to make it work. Vincent would've been Skinny Vinny; Anthony stretched into Bony Tony; Richard made into Rick the Stick; Dean turned into Lean Dean or Lean Cuisine Dean or String Bean Dean or maybe, when someone was looking for a big laugh to impress an eye−rolling high school girl, String Bean Dean the Fat−Burning Machine.

The waiting room is empty, save for me and a woman across from me who is deep in a magazine. She's about my age, with shoulder−length light brown hair and dark eyes behind glasses. The cover shakes as she jiggles crossed legs. I try to focus, to see what she's reading, but all I can see are digitally darkened flesh, splashes of purple and yellow, oversized type promising things that are hot! and sexy! and summer−ready!

"It's only January," I say, without meaning to.

The jiggling stops, and she looks at me. I can read the cover now that it's immobilized: *Summer Fashion: Sexy Ensembles You'll Want to Slip on Stat.* It's only January; why are they talking about summer already? It's too soon for summer, too soon to be stripping off stiff safe denim and loose wool sweaters and protective parkas. Why, in January, must anyone be thinking about bare legs and exposed arms and –

"What?" she says, looking up.

Is she shocked by me? Disgusted? Will she text a friend later to say, *OMG I've never seen anything like it he was like a SKELETON you wouldn't even believe it OMG*?

"Um, never mind," I mumble. The shaking resumes, naked glossy woman on the cover bouncing like she's on a mini-trampoline.

"Carla?" a white-smocked nurse calls out, and the woman tosses a pen on the table and springs off through swinging doors.

I pick up the magazine and flip to the table of contents. This issue promises to bare celebrity baby bumps, share low-calorie summer cocktails, and reveal the weirdest places readers have had sex.

I wonder if those places include a pet cemetery, or a country club golf course, or the stacks of a public library. I think of Bobby's bachelor party last month, where he and Andy and Dougie tried to outdo one another as we sipped smooth whiskey and smoked slow cigars in a five-star hotel suite. The four of us have been best friends since grade school, and Bobby's the first to get married.

"No no no," Bobby's brother Larry had barked, lips wet with warm chocolate from a $5 minibar Snickers, "I did it in an airplane bathroom with – wait for it! – a stewardess. And I plowed her – wait for it! – from behind. Yes, boys: I am a card-carrying member of the mile-high club, so I beat all you assholes."

"You're a pig," Bobby said.

"You're just jealous," Larry informed him. "Hey, Slim Jim, what about you? Want to try and one-up that? What's the wildest place you ever done it? Skinny little guy like you, you coulda nailed two-three stewardesses in the airplane john! All of ya shoved in there at once. Ha!"

There had been a long moment of silence, then I'd set down my crystal tumbler too hard and laughed. "Oh, no; you're right. You win. No one can beat that."

"Watch you don't break that glass," Barry had said, burping and weaving off toward the bathroom. "If you can't hold it with your skinny girly wrists, we'll call down and see about getting you a sippy cup."

I stared at my arms, at my hands, and felt Bobby and Andy and Dougie not looking at me.

"Sorry, Jim," Bobby had finally said.

"That's okay," I said, but what was he sorry for, really? It isn't his fault I'm still virgin at age 28.

It's 10 minutes past my appointment time. There are occasional bursts of laughter behind the glass windows at check−in, but no one calls me back. I'm still alone in the waiting room, except for an aquarium full of quizzical looking fish. I flip further into the magazine, where I find the monthly quiz. It challenges readers to ask *Are You Confident?* The boxes are marked off already, big swishing Xs in bright purple pen, and at the bottom, '1−10 Points: Doubtful Dater' is circled several times.

"You're never sure you're pretty enough, exciting enough, or sexy enough for a guy," the magazine explains. "Your insecurity is holding you back. Take a risk and you might be pleasantly surprised."

I look at the purple pen on the table and picture the woman from the waiting room. Carla. Her bangs were a little long. Maybe she's overdue for a cut, or maybe she likes to hide behind them a bit. Her jeans were loose and she'd hiked them up when she stood; maybe, unlike the woman on the magazine cover, she isn't the type to flaunt her body. Maybe she's not sure she even likes it.

Maybe she takes off her clothes when she's home alone, and forces herself to stare in the mirror with all the lights on. Maybe she turns off the lights when she can't look any longer, then wraps herself up in towels and cries in the dark.

I remember the way she said, "What?" to me. Was there a quaver in her voice? A falter?

I remember the glasses, not contacts, with thick dark frames. How they swallowed so much of her face. How they made her eyes look far away.

"Jim?" a gravelly voice calls out. "I can take you back now."

I drop the magazine and rise to follow the nurse. Carla comes through the other door and walks toward me.

She's walking toward me, right toward me. "Carla," I say hoarsely, and she stops and looks up at me with a jolt. "Carla," I say again, with nothing after.

Her eyes widen. She leans down to grab the magazine and the purple pen, begins backing away slowly, then faster.

"Jim," the nurse says again, in a louder, even more gravelly voice. "*Jim.*"

"Carla?" I say, but she's gone.

"How are you today?" the nurse says as I follow her. "I'll need to get your weight first. Step up on the scale."

# Casting the Net

## by Joanne Jagoda

As the January sun fades to gloom, Damon Southeby adjusts his high—powered binoculars, keeping his eye on Anne Donaldson's beat up Honda in the second row of the teacher's parking lot. It's a chilly San Francisco afternoon, and he zips up the expensive leather jacket he picked up on his last trip to Istanbul. His boots are handmade in Italy; his dark brown hair is longish and perfectly cut. Damon curses this uncomfortable rental car cramping his 6'1" frame, not his usual luxury wheels. Because he doesn't want to be noticed, it serves his purpose blending in with the cars parked near the school.

Anne Donaldson, fifth grade social studies teacher, erases the blackboard with a furious swipe. Her students were impossible today, rude and inattentive. She felt like telling them to *shove it* and walk out, but she still needs this job. Her twins were only nine when Paul had his fatal heart attack on the basketball court. She had been a stay—at—home mom until then. Not only did she have to deal with his death, but it was a huge shock discovering he had been gambling online, burned through their savings and had even cashed in his life insurance. She had to find a job providing health benefits. Anne had worked at Cabrillo School before she had the twins and was lucky they had an opening.

She grabs quizzes to correct, opens her closet for her purse and parka, groaning when she glimpses herself in the hanging mirror. Tomorrow she turns fifty, and she's been fretting over this birthday for months. Anne traces lines at the corners of her eyes and fluffs her hair that badly needs a cut.

She sighs and closes the closet but pauses at her desk, picking up the picture of her and Paul, in the heart−shaped frame, on roller skates in Golden Gate Park. She'd loved him from the rainy night they met when she was a junior at CAL working at the information desk at the library. He kept badgering her until she agreed to have coffee with him. They became inseparable and married when he finished Hastings Law School.

Anne locks her door and waves to colleagues in the hall wishing her an early "happy birthday". They're taking her out tomorrow night to Perry's for the usual birthday drink.

She unlocks her Honda, tosses her tote bag in the back, starts the car but doesn't move − pounding her palm on the steering wheel.

*Paul damn you. I'm done blaming myself for your heart attack. And I'm done blaming you for your gambling addiction. Enough blame! It's time to move on. This birthday is going to be my fresh start.*

Anne's little tantrum is observed by the attractive man with binoculars in the blue Ford hidden in the shadows across from the teacher's parking lot. Damon Southeby did his job thoroughly and has been collecting information on Anne Donaldson and her seventeen year old twins for three weeks − hacking their computers, email and Facebook accounts and breaking in their house through a back window to hide tiny listening devices and cameras. Finding Anne's diary next to her bed was an unexpected gift. *I bet she's venting about her birthday. Good thing women pour their bloody hearts out in their diaries.*

The Donaldson women would be shocked he knows so much about them and their daily routines. Damon considered different scenarios of how to get involved with Anne, but when he saw the girls browsing dating websites for "older" singles he knew just what he needed to do. He created a website catering to over–forty singles. With pop up ads and fake coupons, the twins were soon hooked into his phony website, and they signed up their mother just as he planned.

He parks across the street from her modest split level to watch and listen on his laptop. Tuesdays and Thursdays, the twins get in around five after Robin's volleyball practice and Cassie's orchestra rehearsal.

Anne unloads her groceries on the kitchen counter, opens a bag of pre–washed salad, adds tomatoes, croutons and cucumbers. She pops the marinating chicken into the oven with some potatoes and sets the table. She pours a glass of white wine and says out loud in front of the hall mirror, "Happy 50th Anne Donaldson."

Anne sips her wine wandering to the family photos crowded on the mantle over the fireplace. Her favorite is the four of them in Maui – sunburned and grinning, in front of a huge sand castle on the beach. Cassie, who is Anne's clone, has wild auburn curly hair and Robin, even at ten, was six inches taller and blonde like her dad with a cute sprinkle of freckles. Ever the joker, she was making rabbit ears behind her sister. Raising them as a single parent has been a roller coaster ride. Cassie had a bout of depression and Robin hung with the wrong crowd for a while, but somehow the three of them have made it.

She sees the picture of the girls when they were twelve in Disneyland with their grandparents. She says a silent prayer of thanks for George and Lillian. They adore their only grandchildren, and the twins love spending lazy weekends at their home in Hillsborough, with the big pool and tennis court, where the weather is much warmer than San Francisco.

Without George and Lillian's financial help, she wouldn't have made it. Anne didn't want to tell them about Paul's online gambling but broke down when they hounded her over why he let his insurance lapse. Even though they can be overbearing, they were generous and set up trust funds for the twins to cover the double tuition hit coming up in September. George owns a top secret research facility in the Silicon Valley that he doesn't like to talk about but has made him lots of money.

The girls come in like two cyclones. "Hi Mom," they yell and head upstairs trying to hide a pink cake box. They've become close in the last few years but they went through a stage when they couldn't stand each other.

"Hey kids. How was your day? Dinner in twenty. I made Southwest Chicken."

Robin shouts, "Yum ... and don't forget ... Donaldson Family Meeting tonight!" Anne created this ritual after Paul died for going over important family business. After dinner, Cassie clears the dishes, and Robin brings in a chocolate fudge cake from Anne's favorite bakery, with six lit candles.

The girls sing, then hand her a large white envelope and say together, "Mom, don't open it yet."

Robin raps on the table. "I'm calling this meeting to order." Anne smiles at her daughter, who has turned into a lanky Gwyneth Paltrow with a purple streak in her blonde hair; eyes outlined in black, wearing torn jeans, acting like a corporate CEO.

Cassie, in a plaid skirt and dark tights, chews her thumbnail, which she does when she's nervous and tosses her curly auburn hair. She clears her throat, "Mom, we're starting college next fall. It's time for you to get out." She nods at her sister like they've rehearsed this.

Robin continues, "We're talking about *dating*. We signed you up on an online dating site for singles over forty." She gives her sister a high five.

Anne takes a big bite of chocolate cake. "Online dating? I don't know. I've heard you have to be so careful and ..."

139

"Mom, come on … you have to give it a try. Dina's aunt met someone nice online." Robin opens her laptop. "Here's your profile: *Attractive widow, wants to see foreign films, discover neighborhood restaurants, and hike in the Marin headlands.*"

Anne wipes away a tear. *They know me so well and zeroed in on things I haven't done that I used to love. I think I'm ready for this.*

Cassie points to the envelope. "Open it Mom. We decided … you're lookin' a little 1980's …"

She holds the gift certificate like it's a proclamation then reads it out loud: "Complete Makeover: haircut, massage and makeup application at *Sheer Pleasure.*" Then she laughs. "Wow kids. That's a swanky salon. How did you get the money for this?"

Robin is exasperated, "Duh … we robbed Wells Fargo. Mom, give us a little credit. We do have part time jobs."

Outside in his car, Damon Southeby shakes his hand in the air and yells, "yes!" He's been watching this heartwarming scene unfold on his laptop and smirks because his plan is taking shape. He drives off thinking about the expensive dinner he is going to have tonight to celebrate, courtesy of the wealthy employers in the Middle East he'll update in the morning.

Friday, 31$^{st}$ January 2014

# Palm Valley Moms' Group

## by h. l. nelson

Dear Diary,

Can I call you that? It seems a bit childish, but also awesome! I
haven't had a diary since freshman year of high school. Then
stepmom read it and that put an end to that. She slept in my bed
for two months, because I wrote about how I snuck Andrew
Madison in my window. Oops. I remember I would write my
name all bubbly, with his last name. Then I crossed it out and
put Drew Lufstetter's, when I liked him more. I did not like the
name, though. Joan Lufstetter. Ew. What a cat–lady name that
would have been.

So, as a New Year's resolution (yes, I know I'm late), I've
decided to begin this diary and only write on the 31$^{st}$. Which
means I don't have to write in it every month. (See, I'm smart.) I
just need an outlet. And Mom won't be reading this one,
thankfully.

I'm so glad Christmas is over. But, of course, Anne is already
preparing for this year's party. Let me tell you what happened
earlier today.

I let myself into the unlocked front door of Anne's mansion,
where we meet for our Palm Valley Moms' Group. I strode past
the marble columns and planters of bougainvillea and entered
through the solid mahogany door. Anne was in the middle of a

story about her "amazing" new artichoke soufflé recipe, though she doesn't cook. Ailsa, her personal chef, was serving truffle finger cakes when I walked in. I would have called Anne on it, but I was in a good mood this morning since Rob made love to me for a full ten minutes before heading to work. Ten minutes? you say. Hey, I'll take what I can get.

Anne was saying, "... have to make sure to whip it just so, or it won't come out perfectly, like mine — Well hello, Joan, love. It's good to see you, even though we've already begun our refreshments. Here, sit, and I'll have Ailsa serve you yours."

She flashed her perfectly polished smile in my direction. I wanted to grab the platter of finger cakes and smash it against that infuriating smile.

Her husband makes more than all our husbands, combined. And she loves to flaunt it all. From her drapes, custom-made and shipped from France, to her bleached asshole. (Drunk one night at a martini bar downtown, she told us all about it.)

Anne is one of those rich, driven moms. In their home gyms with personal trainers. Couture workout gear. Headbands. Running shoes. Constant multi-tasking on PDAs or iPads while completing strict regimens. Stair-stepping. Treadmill. Light weights. Alternated with various classes. Pilates. Spinning. Zumba. Asses hard as rocks. If Anne's husband wants anal one night and she doesn't, there's no way in hell he's getting past those buns of steel. Access. Denied.

She ships her outfits from overseas. On occasion, she slums it up at Burberry, while the rest of the group digs in the trenches at Macy's and Old Navy. Even Anne's three girls are picture-perfect: lush symmetrical features, slender tanned legs, and tight bodies. They're straight-A students, vastly talented at ballet, debate, the mandolin. Seriously. Her youngest won some music scholarship for Berkeley. I secretly hope they all end up pregnant before 18.

Anne isn't as perfect as she seems, though. I snooped in her bathroom cabinets one day and saw a bunch of pill bottles. I mean, we all take pills, but this was ridiculous. Vicodin. Percocet. Valium. Xanax. Adderall. What kind of doctor would prescribe all that? She could be a dealer.

*I'm not snooping*, I told myself, as I closed the cabinet door, *I'm a friend and I need to know if Anne has a pill problem.*

Ailsa handed me finger cakes and a cherry vodka sour and I sat down and glanced around the room to see who was there. Julie, at the kitchen bar with her nervous looks and smiles. I like Julie. Her problem's her husband. He's an obsessive−compulsive freak. Their house has to be spotless. Everything in all cabinets, including the medicine cabinets, has to be organized to the nth degree: by height, color, and size. It's ridiculous. He probably has a small penis.

Julie's house has five bedrooms and four bathrooms, so she wakes up at 4 A.M. every day and cleans and organizes, placing kitchen, bathroom, powder room items on their respective shelves in precisely the correct places, labels facing outward. Her kids have learned they can treat her like a pushover, always asking her to make extra food, take inane trips to the mall or grocery store, and wash their clothes right before school, with no thanks. It's no wonder she's so nervous. I see her pull strands of her own hair out when she thinks no one is looking. Poor thing.

The only other one there, lounging on Anne's chaise lounge, was Robin the alcoholic. When she drinks, she's fun − the life of the party, bantering, making cocktails, daring us to do outrageous things like run down the street naked while reciting Shakespeare. Otherwise, she's sullen and scathing, making unfunny cracks at everyone. Which I don't really mind, but the other women can't handle her at those times, they become silent and look meaningfully at each other, like, "No, I said something to her last time. Your turn." Luckily, she usually has a drink in her hand. At one of Anne's dinner parties last year, she turned off the music and announced that her magic show was about to begin. When everyone quieted down, she dropped her pants, spread her legs, and tried to give herself a Goldschläger enema in the middle of Anne's living room. My husband and I pulled her out of the room and helped her dress. All of us, except Anne, laughed about it for months. Honestly, I think Robin drinks to fight off loneliness. Her husband travels a lot. Commodities or trade securities. Some bullshit like that. Really boring. I think he cheats on her while traveling. It's a damn shame.

Robin was banging back a whiskey. She likes 'manly' drinks, and she drinks them fast. I'm sure Robin's liver's destroyed. It really doesn't matter. In the ultimate scheme of things, we're all slowly rotting away in our designer 'mom jeans'.

I swear, it seems like we blinked, then we were through our hot years and into MILF and cougar−land, despite desperate attempts to hang onto our youth. Apparently, growing old means you watch your ass slowly spread. But not like a decadent soft cheese. More like an angry oil spill that no one has the time, and few have the money, to clean up. Skin slowly wrinkling and sliding off faces that boyfriends once gazed at for hours. Vaginas, dried and shriveled prunes. Hormones worse than a teenager's. Breasts going down quicker than the Titanic. Hair sprouting where none should ever grow.

In other societies, we would be matriarchs, prized for our wisdom and prowess. In America, we're just dried−up old whores. Only good for chauffeuring around spoiled, drugged−out, and oversexed teens; concocting elaborate dinner parties where we flirt too much and give our neighbor's husband head in the garage; and wear skimpy swimsuits (once we have our stretch marks lasered, tummies tucked, and Brazilians done) while seducing the pool boy.

Being middle−aged in America sucks. You're in−between your "prime" and cookie baking. Your body is falling apart and you still don't know who the fuck you are. It's the new tweens.

At some point, Anne said, "All right, ladies, we need to talk about the Winter Wonderland neighborhood party."

"What do we need to talk about?" Robin spat. Julie chewed her nails at the kitchen bar.

A smile glazed across Anne's face, as if she was speaking to a child, and she answered, "Well, honey, we need to decide whom is to take care of what tasks." Anne uses the word 'whom' even when it isn't correct. "As you know, this is a very important event and if all doesn't go as planned, the whole neighborhood will blame me. You ladies don't want that to happen, right?"

Anne beamed her fake smile around the room. I thought her brilliant, lasered teeth might sear our retinas if we didn't agree. Julie nodded, as if she wanted to shake loose her own teeth.

"OK, at least that's settled. Now, how about if I just assign everyone their tasks. I think it will go more smoothly if we just do that," Anne said.

So there it was. All along, she had wanted to tell us what to do. Such a surprise. So much bullshit. I drowned my groan in my cherry vodka sour. It was going to be a long day.

And it *was* a long day. Quite long. But, I must be off to bed. Maybe a hot bath will help. Talk to you in a few months, diary.

Not–Anne's–Bitch,

Joan

# Authors

**Rachel Ambrose** is a twenty–something fiction writer from Connecticut. Her favorite season is winter, she enjoys well–made Manhattans, and she loves Southern fiction. Her work has appeared in *Crack the Spine*, *Exiles Literary Magazine*, and *The Colton Review*. She is currently at work on her second novel and blogs at http://victorywhiskeyjuliet.tumblr.com.

**Lynn Beighley** is a fiction writer stuck in a technical book writer's body. Her stories often involve deeply flawed characters and the unsatisfying meshing of the virtual and actual world. She has an MFA in Creative Writing and currently has 16 books published.

**Margaret Bingel** is just a writer, living in Manchester, New Hampshire. She spends her time working at her father's beer store, art modeling, and writing (when she can). She doesn't have a website or a blog yet, but who knows, maybe she'll have one in the future.

**Guilie Castillo–Oriard** is a Mexican writer currently exiled in the island of Curaçao. She misses Mexican food and Mexican *amabilidad*, but the laissez–faire attitude and the beaches of the Caribbean are fair exchange. Plus, the bounty of cultural diversity inspires great culture–clash fiction. Guilie is currently revising and editing her first novel. Her short stories have appeared in *Fiction 365*, *Lady Ink Magazine* and *Pure Slush*. She blogs at http://guilie–castillo–oriard.blogspot.com.

**John Wentworth Chapin** lives and writes in Baltimore, where he is too frequently starting Project B before finishing Project A. John writes non–fiction as well as fiction. Find him on the web at http://johnwentworthchapin.com.

**James Claffey** hails from County Westmeath, Ireland, and lives on an avocado ranch in Carpinteria, CA with his family. He is the author of a collection of short fiction, *Blood a Cold Blue*. His website can be found at http://jamesclaffey.com.

**Gay Degani** has published online and in print including *The Best of Every Day Fiction* editions and her own collection, *Pomegranate Stories*. She is the founder–editor emeritus of EDF's *Flash Fiction Chronicles*, a staff editor at *Smokelong Quarterly*, and blogs at http://wordsinplace.blogspot.com where a list of her work can be found. She's had two stories nominated for Pushcart consideration and won the eleventh Annual Glass Woman Prize for her flash piece, *Something about L.A.*.

**Michelle Elvy** is an editor and writer who has meandered from the shores of the Chesapeake to New Zealand's Bay of Islands. Michelle has published poetry, short stories and non–fiction about travel, faraway places, food, motorcycling, slow travel, the kindness of strangers and raising children in unusual places for numerous literary journals and magazines in the US, Canada, Australasia, the UK and Europe. She edits at *Flash Frontier: An Adventure in Short Fiction* and *Blue Five Notebook*. She can also be found regularly at *Awkword Paper Cut*. More about manuscript assessment and Michelle's take on editing and writing can be found at http://michelleelvy.com.

**Gloria Garfunkel** is the daughter of two Auschwitz survivors, which deeply affected her whole life and personality. She has a Ph.D. from Harvard University in Psychology and Social Relations, concentrating on Personality Development Studies. She was a psychotherapist for thirty years working with children, adults and families. She is currently retired, reading and writing to her heart's content. She has published many stories in journals and anthologies and hopes to eventually publish a collection of her flash fiction. You can find more of her work at her blog http://queruloussquirreldaily.blogspot.com/.

**Teresa Burns Gunther** has had fiction and non−fiction appear in numerous literary journals and most recently in *Northwind Magazine, Bookslut* and *Best New Writing 2012.* Teresa is the Editor of *The Lakeside*, an online literary magazine, and she founded Lakeshore Writers Workshop in Oakland, California where she leads creative writing workshops and classes and works one−on−one with writers. You can find links to her work at http://www.teresaburnsgunther.com/.

**Gill Hoffs** lives with her family and an ever−dwindling supply of Nutella in the North of England. Find Gill on Facebook or as @gillhoffs on twitter, email her a dirty joke at gillhoffs@hotmail.co.uk, or leave a clean comment at http://gillhoffs.wordpress.com/. *Wild: a collection* was published by *Pure Slush Books* in 2012. Her non−fiction book *The Sinking of RMS Tayleur: the Lost Story of the Victorian Titanic* is out now from *Pen & Sword.* Feel free to send her chocolate.

**Joanne Jagoda** of Oakland, California, took an inspiring writing workshop after retiring in 2009, and launched on a long−postponed creative writing journey. Since discovering her passion for writing, she has worked non−stop on short stories, poetry and non−fiction. Her work has appeared in a number of e−zines and print anthologies, including *Pure Slush* and *Idea*

*Gems Magazine*, and she was a poet of the month for a Jewish news weekly in Northern California. When not taking writing and poetry classes, Joanne enjoys being a writer–coach for ninth graders, Zumba, and visiting her three grandchildren in Jerusalem.

**Len Kuntz** is a writer from Washington State and an editor at the online literary magazine *Metazen*. His work appears widely in print and online. Find him at http://lenkuntz.blogspot.com.

**Sally–Anne Macomber** was born and raised in Toronto, Canada, and studied journalism at Concordia University in Montreal. Her work on high fashion and the demise of haute couture has appeared in various online and print publications in both Europe and North America. She turned to writing flash fiction in 2010, and hasn't looked back.

**Jessica McHugh** is an author of speculative fiction that spans the genre from horror and alternate history to epic fantasy. A member of the Horror Writers Association and a 2013 Pulp Ark nominee, she has devoted herself to novels, short stories, poetry, and playwriting. Jessica has had thirteen books published in five years, including the bestselling *Rabbits in the Garden*, *The Sky: The World* and the gritty coming–of–age thriller, *PINS*. More info on her speculations and publications can be found at http://www.jessicamchughbooks.com.

**Gwendolyn Joyce Mintz** is a fiction writer and aspiring photographer. Her work has appeared in various online and print publications. In other incarnations, Mintz is a writing instructor, a teddy bear maker and somebody's grandmother.

**h. l. nelson** is Founding Editor/Executive Director of *Cease, Cows* lit mag and a former sidewalk mannequin. Pub credits: *PANK, Hobart, Connotation Press, Metazen, Drunk Monkeys,*

*Red Fez, Bartleby Snopes*. She's also editing an anthology which includes stories by Aimee Bender, Roxane Gay, Lindsay Hunter and other fierce women writers. Her MFA is currently kicking her ass. Tell her what you're wearing: heather@hlnelson.com.

**Mandy Nicol** grew up in Melbourne, Australia and made a tree change to country Victoria in the mid—nineties – the decade, not her age. She has various animals including a flockette of pet sheep that are thankful for her vegaquarian habits. She writes short stories and loves flash fiction. *Pure Slush* is the first venue to publish her work.

**Derek Osborne** lives in eastern Pennsylvania. His work has appeared in *Boston Literary Magazine*, *Bartleby Snopes*, *Literary Orphans*, *The Linnet's Wings*, *Pure Slush* and many others. To read more visit http://gertrudesflat.blogspot.com, or email him at derekosborne1@gmail.com.

**Vanessa Weibler Paris** lives in Erie, Pa., with a guy, a girl, a boy, a bunny rabbit and a dog. She writes things both real (for work) and pretend (for fun). Her favorite things include hot peppers, bad puns, small—world stories, and tales with a twist at the end.

**Gary Percesepe** is Associate Editor at *New World Writing* (formerly *Mississippi Review*) and a Contributor at *The Nervous Breakdown*. Author of four books in philosophy, Percesepe's poetry, fiction, essays, and interviews have appeared in *Story Quarterly*, *N + 1*, *Salon*, *Mississippi Review*, *The Millions*, *Brevity*, *PANK*, *Metazen*, *The Brooklyner*, and other places. His collection of short stories, *Why I Did the Grocery Girl*, is forthcoming from Aqueous Books. His poetry collection *falling* and his flash fiction collection *itch* were published by *Pure Slush Books* in late 2013. He has taught at Saint Louis University, Wittenberg University, and University of Dayton. He lives in

Buffalo, New York.

**Matt Potter** is an Australian–born writer who keeps a part of his psyche in Berlin. Matt has been published in various places online, and he is, rather amazingly, also the founding editor of *Pure Slush*. You can find more of his work at his website: http://mattcpotter.webs.com/.

**Darryl Price** was born in Kentucky and educated at Thomas More College. A founding member of L. Jack Roth's Yellow Pages Poets, he has published dozens of chapbooks, and his poems have appeared in many journals. He currently edits *Olentangy Review* with his wife Melissa.

**Stephen V. Ramey** is an American author from New Castle, Pennsylvania. His work has appeared in many places, including *The Doctor TJ Eckleburg Review*, *The Journal of Compressed Creative Arts*, and *A Capella Zoo*. *Glass Animals*, his first collection of (very) short fiction is available from *Pure Slush Books*. Find him and more of his work at his website: http://www.stephenvramey.com.

**Shane Simmons** is a self–confessed coffee shop writer who believes that regardless of quality, each paragraph penned should be rewarded with sweet treats (cake, muffins, Belgian waffles, etc). London–born, he ran away to Glasgow ten years ago. Since then he has expanded his waistline and he now blogs at http://scribblingsimmons.wordpress.com/.

**Kimberlee Smith** is a writer whose poetry, essays, fiction, and creative non–fiction have been published in numerous literary journals and anthologies. She was awarded a residency to the Jentel Arts Program in 2013. She lives with her two daughters, two dogs, three cats, two rabbits, and nine chooks on her farm in rural Connecticut. She received her MA in English from the

University of Sydney, a certificate in the Creative Writing Program through UCLA, and her BA in Journalism from the University of Southern California. She is enrolled currently in post−graduate studies at Columbia University in New York. She can do a headstand on a trampoline, kill a chook, and make hard cider from the apples in her orchard.

**Andrew Stancek** was born in Bratislava and saw Russian tanks occupying his homeland. His dreams of circuses and ice cream, flying and lion−taming, miracle and romance have appeared recently in print in *LA Review, Windsor Review* and *New Sun Rising: Stories for Japan.* Among the many online publications featuring his work are *Every Day Fiction, Gemini Magazine* (Flash Fiction Contest Grand Prize Winner), *fwriction, r.kv.r.y. quarterly literary journal, Tin House, Flash Fiction Chronicles, The Linnet's Wings, Connotation Press, THIS Literary Magazine, LA Review, Windsor Review, Thrice Fiction Magazine, New Sun Rising,* and *Pure Slush.*

**Susan Tepper** is the author of four published books of fiction and a chapbook of poetry. Her most recent title *The Merrill Diaries* (*Pure Slush Books*, July 2013) is a Novel in Stories that follow a young woman's adventures in love and lust on two continents, spanning a decade. Tepper has received nine Pushcart nominations, and one for the Pulitzer Prize in fiction. You can visit her website here: http://www.susantepper.com.

**Nathaniel Tower** lives in the Twin Cities with his wife and daughter. After teaching high school English for nine years, he decided to pursue a career in writing / publishing / editing. His fiction has appeared in over two hundred online and print journals. His first collection of fiction, *Nagging Wives, Foolish Husbands,* was released in 2013 through *Martian Lit.* Nathaniel is the founding and managing editor of *Bartleby Snopes Literary Magazine and Press.* Find out more about Nathaniel at http://nathanieltower.wordpress.com.

**Townsend Walker** lives in San Francisco. His stories have been published in over fifty literary journals and included in seven anthologies. One story won the SLO NightWriters story contest. Two were nominated for the PEN / O. Henry Award. Four were performed at the New Short Fiction Series in Hollywood. He is associate editor at *Grey Sparrow Journal*. During a career in finance he published three books, on foreign exchange, derivatives and portfolio management. Educated at Georgetown, NYU and Stanford, you can find his website at http://www.townsendwalker.com.

**Michael Webb** is continually surprised anyone is interested in what he has to say, and he blogs occasionally at http://innocentsaccidentshints.blogspot.com.

# Other anthologies from Pure Slush

Visit the Pure Slush Store:
http://pureslush.webs.com/store.htm

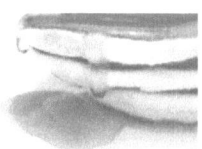

**February 2014 Vol. 2**
ISBN: 978−1−925101−14−0

**March 2014 Vol. 3**
ISBN: 978−1−925101−17−1

**April 2014 Vol. 4**
ISBN: 978−1−925101−27−0

**May 2014 Vol. 5**
ISBN: 978−1−925101−30−0

## barcode
### Pure Slush Vol. 8
ISBN: 978-1-925101-00-3
There's something wonderfully sleazy — and levelling — about bars and bar stories. They certainly don't *have* to be sleazy but there's always the possibility that a bit of alcohol and some smoking and hair let down and belts loosened can lead to candour and laughter and exposé …

Don't glug these stories down all in a single session: give each one the savouring and the contemplation it deserves. Too much, too soon? No one likes a sloppy drunk!

*Originally published August 2013*


## Catherine refracted
### Pure Slush Vol. 7
ISBN: 978-1-304-12272-8
Legands abound about Catherine the Great, Empress and Autocrat of All the Russias.

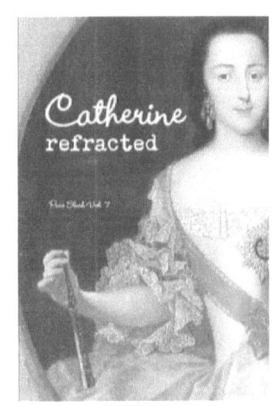

*Catherine refracted* is a re-imagining of the life and the legends of Catherine the Great. Her lovers, her illegitimate children, her wiles, her wit and her place in history … all feature in this lively reinterpretation of one of history's most beloved and reviled leaders. Featuring the work of nineteen writers, including rare juvenilia and modern reappraisals of Catherine the Great's place in world cultural history.

*Originally published June 2013*

## obit. Pure Slush Vol. 6

ISBN: 978−1−300−86001−3

Webster Murphy Allen 1925 – 2012. Lawyer, opera−goer, philanthropist, father, grandfather, generous with his time and talents and money ... or was he?

*obit.* explores the many sides of a man many people *thought* they knew. Each writer has taken an incident or anecdote or memory from Webster's life and created a fully−fleshed man with multiple quirks ... and maybe even multiple secrets. Where does the truth lie?

Featuring thirty−two different stories by twenty−two different writers.                    *Originally published March 2013*

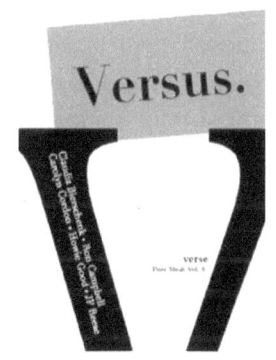

## Versus. Pure Slush Vol. 5

ISBN: 978−1−300−76169−3

Can good poetry be written on demand? The answer is "Yes" and *Versus.* is the proof.

*Bill Yarrow*

5 poets write 15 poems each against 15 different topics – drink, seasons, convenience stores, marriage, chores, personal grooming, budgets, interior decoration, gender, public transport, church, raising children, politics, guilty pleasures, future – so the collection features 75 different opinions. All are different and unique in their own way.

*Originally published February 2013*

gorge: a novel in stories
Pure Slush Vol. 4
ISBN: 978-1-300-54979-6
Fifty-four stories told by thirty-three writers. Each story is a chapter in the tale of the misplaced Café Gano, a restaurant in a small town on the Maine coast.

The action takes place over one day, and as the afternoon progresses and the evening unfolds, customers' lives unravel and staff decorum snaps to erupt in a crescendo of miscalculated faith and desperate bids for ultimate control. Yeah, it's that crazy!!

For any person who has ever worked in a restaurant, or been a patron, you will laugh aloud at the follies, wonder who will hook up with whom, and at the pace I read this, ask yourself, when will *Pure Slush* bring out the next novel of compilations?
*Robert Vaughan*

Recommended, particularly if you appreciate a bold experiment in narrative and variety of perspective.      *Stephen V. Ramey*
*Originally published December 2012*

**real Pure Slush Vol. 3**
ISBN: 978-1-291-14109-2
upfront! uptight! up-yours! Cutting edge non-fiction from thirty-one writers who spill their guts on life and love, sex and travel, food and legalities and freedom and family, reflecting the true diversity of everyday experience.
*Originally published October 2012*

**Notausgang: emergency exit**
**Pure Slush Vol. 2**
ISBN: 978−1−4717−0059−0

Stories desperate and amusing, based on the theme *emergency exit*. Scary, creepy, funny, illuminating, sad and life−affirming. Twenty−four stories, fiction and non−fiction.

Every story in this collection, while based on the same theme, is well−crafted, rich in the detail of countless settings, and full of interesting and unique characters, each with their own journey through life, with all its unpredictable twists and turns. All the stories are short ones, yet each contains their characters' lifetimes and then some − each seeking some type of 'emergency exit' in their own way.
*Joyce Juzwik*

*Originally published May 2012*

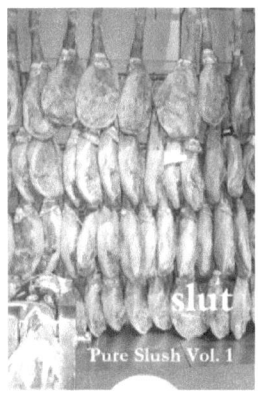

**slut Pure Slush Vol. 1**
**(2nd edition)**
ISBN: 978−1−4716−0674−8

a zesty, amusing (and serious) anthology of fiction and non−fiction on the theme 'slut' … where it all began!!

*Originally published February 2012*

For the complete range of Pure Slush
print books and eBooks, visit the Pure Slush Store at
http://pureslush.webs.com/store.htm.